HER BOLDEST LIE

A ROSEMARY RUN THRILLER

KELLY UTT

STANDARDS
OF STARLIGHT

2019 Standards of Starlight Paperback Edition

www.standardsofstarlight.com

ISBN: 978-1-7337712-4-5

Cover art by Justin Carolyne

PROLOGUE

It was a cold November night when Marcheline Fay last saw the man she claimed had fathered her only child. She had left him under the cover of darkness, having stuffed everything she owned into an old Ford Pinto and driven away. If she closed her eyes, she could still feel the biting wind and the weight of the bags in her hands, her pulse racing faster than the rhythm of the rustling leaves. She'd barely made it out without being caught.

Evanston, Illinois was a leafy suburb north of Chicago with good schools and low crime. It was everything Marcheline's parents had dreamed of before the family emigrated from France when she was a baby. Soon after arriving in the United States, they had opened a bakery selling traditional recipes from their homeland and were living the American dream. Marcheline had grown up lonely since her parents were at work most of the time, but it had been a small price to pay for financial stability and more room to stretch than they'd had back in Paris. Her parents loved her. She knew that. But something had been missing.

Her mother had warned her about getting involved with a boy from the wrong side of the tracks. And the warnings weren't without merit. There had been gang activities, alcohol and drug addictions, and violence to contend with. Grim stories filled the nightly news. But Marcheline had gotten involved with such a boy, anyway. She thought she'd known better. After all, she had spent most of her life in America, and there was a lot that her French parents just didn't understand.

Marcheline was barely seventeen when Chester Loor had charmed her, his handsome features and rich brown skin, darker than her own, standing out as compared to the light-skinned kids who filled the streets of her neighborhood and the halls of her school. Chester had seemed exotic. Maybe it was because Marcheline longed to be in better touch with her African roots. Or maybe she just wanted to be with someone who looked like she did. Whatever the reason, she had thrown caution to the wind, sneaking out with Chester against her parents' wishes and without their knowledge. He had turned out to be just as bad for Marcheline as her mother had predicted. And then some.

Now, as an adult with a grown daughter of her own, Marcheline wasn't proud of her choices during that time in her life. In fact, she tried not to ever think about them. She had turned things around for herself and little Sabine, moving to Northern California, attending college, and eventually settling in the quaint town of Rosemary Run and opening a winery. It had been difficult to accomplish so much as a single mother, but Marcheline had persevered, following in her parents' footsteps and emulating their strong work ethic. She had grown Maison du Vin to be one of the most successful wineries in the region, entertaining tourists from around the world and exporting bottles of her product nearly as far.

Things had been close enough to perfect. Until Sabine got married, had a baby of her own, and grew curious about the man who had given her life. At odds with Marcheline on getting in contact with her father, one day on a whim, Sabine found a sealed envelope in her mother's belongings addressed to a mystery recipient named C.M. Loor in Chicago, Illinois. Acting hastily and without asking for Marcheline's permission, Sabine added a stamp to the envelope and dropped it into a blue mailbox stationed outside of the Rosemary Run Post Office. Little did Sabine know, her foolhardy choice would soon threaten to destroy Marcheline Fay's carefully constructed life and endanger them all.

1

Oblivious to the danger that awaited her, Marcheline was enjoying a productive morning in the office. She was seated at her desk on the winery grounds, overlooking her two-hundred-thirty acres of rolling vineyard. She'd had the perfect picture window specially constructed a few years prior when she had left her original, smaller office building and commissioned the new headquarters.

Business was booming, so Marcheline didn't feel guilty about spending extra for the luxury she enjoyed. She was in a place in her life where she had enough savings and assets to provide a cushion even if business took a downturn and she had to weather leaner times. She'd had a number in mind and once her net worth surpassed it, she gave herself permission to splurge here and there.

At first, it was hard to get used to spending money on herself for more than the bare essentials. Marcheline had grown-up pinching pennies and watching her spending carefully under her parents exacting eyes. It hadn't happened overnight, but eventually, Marcheline had found herself living more comfortably than she'd ever imagined. Luxuries like heated floors, smart security systems, high-tech kitchen gadgets, and weighted blankets were things she hadn't even dreamed of. But once she tried some of the creature comforts her wealthy friends raved about, Marcheline saw the appeal.

She sometimes felt like Oprah Winfrey, making lists of her favorite things and giving posh gifts to her friends. Oprah hadn't seemed to harbor guilt about enjoying her wealth, Marcheline reasoned, which made her an ideal woman to look up to. Oprah had worked hard, just like Marcheline, and by all accounts deserved the money she'd earned. Marcheline even looked like Oprah, her strong cheekbones, dark skin, sturdy figure, and commanding presence making her hard to ignore. Deciding Oprah was as good an idol as any, Marcheline had followed her example when it came to questions of how to exist as a wealthy woman in this man's world. She had even pretended to be Oprah sometimes, gazing into the mirror and rehearsing affirmations until her own confidence had settled in deep.

On this morning, it was early October and harvest season was in full swing. Marcheline's staff was busy picking grapes and getting them into the fermenter. The fruit was at the peak of ripeness, and this year's harvest looked good. They would make a lot of wine out of the grapes that were being pulled from the vines each and every moment. The entire team was proud of the product. And the employees were happy.

Marcheline was a good boss. She offered higher than

average wages, and she provided generous healthcare benefits and paid time off. Most of her employees had been with her for more than a decade, which she thought spoke to their loyalty and dedication to the business. If they hadn't been happy, they wouldn't have stayed. There were plenty of other wineries in the region they could have worked at instead.

A collection of framed photos on top of Marcheline's desk caught her eye every time she glanced up and out the picture window. Most of the photos featured her daughter, Sabine Fay. Sabine was everything to Marcheline, and she could not have been prouder of Sabine's young family. Sabine and her husband, Ryan Martin, were parents to a healthy baby girl named Amelie. They lived less than five minutes away from Marcheline's estate, and they all saw each other often. Being a grandmother was a greater joy than Marcheline had dared to wish. Family life was good, and they had the photos to prove it.

Marcheline smiled as she glanced from one picture to the next. A square, silver frame held a photo from Sabine and Ryan's wedding, the happy couple beaming with joy as they held up their shiny new wedding rings. A wooden frame next to it held one of Sabine's senior photos from her high school years at East Valley High School. Another featured a five-year-old Sabine sitting on Marcheline's lap as they posed by a Christmas tree, the warm glow of the decorative lights filling the frame. The framed photo beside it showcased a newborn Amelie, pink and healthy, a living symbol of their love and pride. Marcheline could get lost staring at those photos and thinking about how grateful she was for the happy life she had managed to create for her daughter and, by extension, for her baby granddaughter.

Rande Floyd, Marcheline's vice president and right-hand man at Maison du Vin, knocked on her office door, then popped his head inside. "Good morning, Ma'am," Rande said with a crooked smile. Marcheline had told her associate he didn't need to call her ma'am, but he insisted on doing it, anyway. It was part token of respect and part good-natured teasing. It had become a nickname.

"Morning, Rande," Marcheline said. "How are those sales reports coming?"

Rande was a Caucasian man in his late fifties with sun-weathered skin that was beginning to look like leather. He had the air of an old cowboy. Despite his slow drawl, he was smart as a whip. He had been born and raised in Rosemary Run, then had spent two decades in Wyoming working on a cattle ranch. He had married late in life to a younger woman who ended up wanting to put down roots somewhere the kids could grow up knowing their grandparents. When Rande returned to town, Marcheline had been his first stop. He'd heard of the high standards at her winery and knew he wanted to be involved. It took a little convincing, but Marcheline quickly came to understand Rande's charms. In the year since they'd been working together, they had become known as an odd couple in the local business community. On the surface, Rande and Marcheline seemed like opposites, but the differences in their backgrounds only served to benefit their partnership. Rande had a good head on his shoulders. Marcheline relied on him to be the voice of reason and to focus on practicality. He had not disappointed her.

"So far, so good," Rande said as he sat down in one of the plush yellow chairs in front of Marcheline's desk. As usual, he looked out of place against her stylish office decor. Rande tapped one finger on his bottom lip like he always did when he was thinking. He tapped the toe of his polished cowboy boot in rhythm. "I'm pleased."

The company had recently begun exporting to Europe and Marcheline was eager to learn how the new exports were impacting the bottom line. The cost of shipping wine bottles overseas was enough to make her skeptical about the long-term viability of the new venture. She wanted to be sure Maison du Vin would earn enough to make the higher costs worth the trouble. It was the biggest risk she had taken in business.

"Are we in the black yet?" Marcheline asked. "I know it will take some time to turn enough profit to offset the overseas shipping expenses, so I will await news of that victory patiently. But as you know, I tend to get on edge while I wait." She looked at Rande, considering their situation. "You promised me this expansion would be a roaring success. Do you still stand by that?"

"Promise is a strong way of putting it," Rande said with a cautious grin. "But I'm doing my very best for you, Ma'am. You have my word on that."

"Good enough," Marcheline confirmed. She knew Rande was indeed a man of his word and wouldn't use the term promise lightly. "What else is happening this morning? Any updates on the harvest?"

They both glanced out the picture window.

Marcheline thought her new office reminded her of the bridge of a ship. It was a command center of sorts. She thought it an honor to sit at the helm.

"Things are looking good out there, Ma'am," Rande said in his deep, gruff voice. "I just ran the numbers and I project we will exceed last year's harvest by a good margin."

"That's fabulous news," Marcheline replied. "Nothing would make me happier."

"Other than that grandbaby of yours," Rande added. "How's the little rugrat doing?"

Marcheline laughed. "Right as usual, my friend," she replied. She leaned back in her reclining chair, her curly hair billowing around her shoulders. "Little Amelie is just the best. I highly recommend getting a grandbaby of your own someday."

"Hey, now," Rande replied. "I've got a ways to go before that happens. I'm still in the thick of the elementary school years with my own kids. Charisse stays busy with after-school activities, homework, and volunteering at the school."

Marcheline remembered those days like they were yesterday. "Charisse is a good one. You're a lucky man."

"You don't have to tell me. I know that like I know my own name. The only thing I don't know is how I talked her into marrying me in the first place."

They laughed together. Marcheline appreciated the ease with which she and Rande could converse.

In addition to being colleagues, Marcheline and Rande were true friends. Rande understood Marcheline and everything she had been through like few other people did. Over the years they'd worked together, they had spent a lot of hours talking. Marcheline had even told him a good deal about her life before moving to California. In fact, she had told him more than she had her closest girlfriends. Something about Rande made him easy to talk to. He seemed trustworthy, like he'd take your secrets to his grave. He was old-school like that.

"Speaking of lucky men," Rande continued. "How are things going with the new guy? Hasn't he been around long enough now that I might get some details?"

"What?" Marcheline asked, lowering her head and pretending not to know what he was talking about. "You're the only man in my life, Rande. Well, other than Limbo the coonhound, that is."

"And you still don't think there is a deeper meaning behind the fact that you named your dog Limbo?" Rande asked. "Maybe the name reflects the status of your love life?"

Marcheline chuckled. "I told you, Rande. I named him after the limbo dance. It was innocent, I promise."

"Okay, then," Rande muttered. "Are you trying to convince me? Or yourself?"

"Oh, hush."

"Certainly, Ma'am," Rande teased. "Just as soon as you tell me about the new guy, I'll stand up and march right back down to my own office, where I'll remain for the rest of the morning, hushed. And *that's* a promise."

Marcheline was guarded about her love life. During Sabine's childhood, she hadn't dated at all. Marcheline hadn't felt like she was available to give herself to someone in that way. She hadn't trusted herself, and she didn't want to get Sabine mixed up in any unnecessary drama. And besides, it wasn't as if she had a good track record. She hadn't had a successful romantic relationship in her entire life. Business, she could figure out. Romance was a lot trickier.

"Alright. Fine," Marcheline said reluctantly. "You talked me into it. But Rande, I want you to keep this between us."

"Oh, nice," he replied, standing up and shuffling over to shut the door. "That must mean it's good. I'm all ears, Ma'am."

Marcheline could feel her face getting warm at the thought of talking about her love life. She wished she had more experience. She wished she didn't feel like a middle schooler at her first dance.

"It's embarrassing, Rande."

"No need to be embarrassed. It's just me you're talking to you. What's his name?"

"His name… is Leonard. Leonard Dawson."

"Okay," Rande replied. "We're off to a good start. Where did you meet Leonard Dawson?"

Marcheline ran her thumb along the armrest of her chair nervously as she talked. "At a Chamber of Commerce meeting, actually. He's a banker."

Rande opened his eyes wide and raised his eyebrows. "Highfalutin," he said with a laugh. "That might be good. Someone who can keep up with you."

"Just what is that supposed to mean?" Marcheline asked, teasing back.

"You know what it means," Rande replied. "What does he look like? And how old is he? Tell me the basics."

Marcheline closed her eyes as she pictured Leonard's face. "He's tall, dark, and handsome. I'm not sure exactly how old he is, but around my age."

"How dark are we talking?"

"Skin tone like mine," Marcheline said, amused.

"Does he wear a fancy watch? Like the ones bankers always wear in movies?"

"I guess so, yeah," she replied. "He's serious and intense. Very dedicated to his career. But he's nice. We have fun together."

"I see. Have you done the horizontal mambo yet?"

"Rande!" Marcheline exclaimed, her face getting hotter. "You have no shame."

"I'm simply assessing the situation, Ma'am," he replied. "So, have you?"

Marcheline hesitated. She knew she could trust Rande, but she felt funny talking about sex. So far, she'd kept particulars about her dating life to herself. "Maybe," she answered, coyly.

Rande looked at her, wide-eyed with a smirk on his face. He was waiting, and he would not let her off the hook until she spilled more details.

"Alright, alright," Marcheline said. "Yes. But don't you dare repeat that, Rande."

He gestured, as if zipping his lips. "It's under lock and key."

"But that's not the most surprising part of the story," Marcheline said, winking.

"Do tell, Ma'am. I won't have a need to watch my afternoon soap operas after hearing all of this."

"You're so silly," Marcheline said. She knew Rande

wouldn't be caught dead watching an afternoon soap opera, which made his comment that much funnier. "The most surprising part... Is that there's another man, too. I'm seeing them both."

"Would you look at you?"

"His name is Jim Bennett."

"And what is he like?"

"He is... A lot different from Leonard. Jim is a history teacher at East Valley High. And he's pale as pale can be, with blonde hair and a man bun. He kind of reminds me of a middle-aged surfer dude. A Matthew McConaughey type."

"What do you know?" Rande mused. "I take it Leonard isn't the surfer dude type."

"Not at all," Marcheline said emphatically. "I'd be surprised if he spent much time outdoors. He wouldn't want to get his expensive shoes dirty."

Rande laughed heartily now, placing one leathery hand over his belly. "Sounds like you've got quite the opposite ends of the spectrum in play here. I guess I can see you wanting to sample some different flavors at all. You're still pretty new to this thing called dating."

"Is that what I'm doing? Sampling flavors?"

"You tell me. How do they taste, Ma'am?"

Marcheline grew embarrassed again. "You're terrible," she said to her friend. "But I guess you're right. For whatever reason, I finally got up the courage to try dating. I suppose it feels like my life is stable enough now to try a few things and find out what I like. I'll figure it out in time."

"That's right, you will. And if any of these guys give you trouble, you let me know about it. You hear?"

"That's sweet, Rande. Do you realize you're like a big brother to me? Like the big brother I never had. I sure could have used a big brother's protection when I was a kid."

"I know it, Ma'am. If the position's open, I suppose I'll take it," he replied with a smile. "Truth be told, I already think of you as a kid sister. At first, it was weird that you were also my boss. But we have the kind of friendship that will outlast our professional relationship. It's all good. Don't you think?"

Marcheline crossed her hands in front of her as she smiled back at her friend. "Indeed, it is," she replied. "All good. Now get back to your office and hush. Like you promised. I have work to do."

2

"Yes, hello?" Marcheline answered as she picked up the phone on her desk. "You've reached Maison du Vin. Marcheline Fay speaking."

"Mom, it's me," Sabine said.

"Oh, hello, my darling. What are you doing calling me on this line?"

"I tried your mobile. It went straight to voicemail, which is full, by the way," Sabine explained. "I wondered if you'd like to meet me and Amelie for lunch. Can you get away?"

Sabine was accustomed to her mother's work taking up much of her attention. She knew not to assume Marcheline would be free, especially during harvest season.

"That would be lovely. You know, I always like to see my baby girl and her baby girl. Let me just check my calendar," Marcheline replied. "Where are you thinking?"

"Somewhere quick is fine," Sebine explained. "It won't take long. How about Brick House Cafe? When we're finished, I can get Amelie in the stroller and do some walking around downtown."

"Ah, I see. I can squeeze out an hour. Do you think that will be enough? I'd do more, but with harvest season, it's difficult to get away for long."

"I understand," Sabine confirmed. "You forget, I've been around for many harvest seasons over the years. All of them, actually. So, I get it. And yes, an hour should be enough."

Agreeing to meet her daughter mid-day, Marcheline hung up the phone. She leaned back in her chair, lost in thought.

There had been times as Sabine was growing up when Marcheline had worried she was spending too much time at work, like her own parents had. She had done her best to carve out time with her child, but the demands of growing a business had often meant that parenting took a backseat or that Marcheline was forced to burn the candle at both ends. There had been many days when she had gone home to eat dinner with young Sabine and tuck her into bed, then had stayed up late working until well after midnight only to rise again early the next morning and make her daughter breakfast before school.

Since it had been just the two of them, Marcheline had relied on friends who had become like family to fill in the gaps. A trusted sitter picked up any loose ends. But Marcheline had sometimes wondered how things would turn out for her daughter. She had feared Sabine might go looking for love and attention in the wrong places, much like Marcheline had done herself. She had wanted better for her child. She had focused as much energy as she possibly could on keeping Sabine from feeling lonely like she had. Thankfully, it appeared that Marcheline's efforts had paid off, because not long after Sabine had finished her graphic design degree at the University of Nevada, Las Vegas and ventured into the professional world back home in Rosemary Run, she had chosen a life partner and father for her child who was upstanding and good.

Ryan Martin was a Sanford-trained architect who worked for a reputable local firm in town. His expertise was cutting edge. He focused on green design for structures that were environmentally friendly. He was still young, in his late twenties, but he had already established a reputation as a hard-working creative professional capable of handling both residential and commercial projects. Marcheline planned to have her son-in-law handle the remodel of the building slated to house a new wine store she aimed to open downtown. He had the chops. Marcheline knew she could count on him.

When Sabine met Ryan and learned that he came from a large family, it had made Marcheline feel relieved and happy. Ryan's family had lived in Rosemary Run for three generations. He boasted four siblings, two sets of grandparents, several aunts and uncles, and a slew of cousins, nieces, and nephews, all living nearby. Ryan's family was friendly and welcoming. They'd taken Sabine in as their own in the three years she and Ryan had been together, and Marcheline by extension. Sabine and Ryan were a happy couple. It was the best outcome Marcheline could have wished for her daughter. It was far better than what Marcheline had experienced as a young woman. She thought Sabine's hard-earned happiness was what life should be about, really. To work hard and provide a better life for your child, so that the challenges you faced aren't even on their radar. Marcheline only wished Sabine understood that better.

Lately, Sabine had been quick to criticize Marcheline's decisions, and she seemed determined to dig up old skeletons from the past. Little did Sabine know, Marcheline would fight with everything in her to keep that history hidden. It was too dangerous to bring into the light. She told herself it would be easy to dissuade Sabine, just like it had been when she was a kid and she'd had her mind set on this or that. But deep down, Marcheline knew better. Sabine wanted answers. And she deserved them. Marcheline knew it would be a balancing act.

Brick House Cafe was bustling when Marcheline arrived and placed her hand on one of the large silver door handles out front. Pumpkins flanked the entrance while colorful mums sat in rustic metal pots nearby. It was one of Marcheline's favorite restaurants in town for a quick bite. The exposed-brick walls and city-village vibe had always appealed to her. The cafe had been built into the brick of a taller building and featured large windows around the front three sides. It reminded her a lot of the architecture back in Chicago.

Marcheline didn't talk about Chicago nearly as much as she thought about it. While she actively avoided memories about her time with Chester and tossed those thoughts out when they encroached upon her consciousness, Marcheline often allowed herself to reminisce about earlier portions of her childhood in Illinois.

When she was a kid, Marcheline's parents had taken her to an International Festival in Chicago every fall. They'd spend the day taking in the colorful dress and customs of different cultures from around the world, spending most of their time in the area related to their home country of France. But France wasn't the only country they enjoyed experiencing the culture of. Marcheline's mother had escorted her around the entire festival in the hopes she'd gain an appreciation for the beauty that existed all around the world. When their legs were tired and they were full to the brim with cultural goodness, they'd make their way to a little cafe with exposed brick walls and large windows in the front that looked much like Rosemary Run's very own Brick House Cafe. Marcheline took a breath and enjoyed the happy memories as she looked at the restaurant where she was scheduled to meet her daughter.

As she stepped inside, Marcheline saw Sabine and little Amelie immediately. Sabine was standing in a waiting area just a few feet away while holding Amelie on her hip. The baby was five-months-old now and at the stage where she loved to look around at everything. Mirrors, art and pictures with primary colors, and people's faces provided endless entertainment. Amelie would stare, transfixed and taking it all in. It was a joy to walk her around and show her the world. It was a joy to see the world anew through the baby's eyes.

Amelie noticed Marcheline first, her chubby little face lighting up with recognition as her rosy pink lips formed into a smile. She was happy to see her grandmother, and the feeling was mutual.

"Sabine! My darling," Marcheline said as she leaned forward and kissed her daughter on the cheek. "And Amelie, my little darling. How are you, dear?"

Amelie flung her weight forward towards her grandmother and lifted her arms. She was becoming skilled at expressing her wishes now. Marcheline was grateful that the baby wanted to go to her.

"Hi, Mom," Sabine said, handing the baby over. Amelie squealed with delight as she landed in Marcheline's arms.

"Good," Marcheline said. "Let's get a table."

Sabine took the lead, walking to the hostess stand as Marcheline followed behind. Little Amelie grasped the blue glass beads around her grandmother's neck and examined each one closely.

"Table for two," Sabine said. "And a highchair if you have one."

A young redhead picked up menus and rolls of silverware from behind the stand, then showed the ladies to a booth up against a row of windows.

"Perfect," Marcheline said as she sat down and got Amelie situated on her lap. "This is my favorite view, over the courtyard. I especially love it this time of year with all the colorful leaves on the trees."

"You don't have to hold her if you don't want to, Mom," Sabine said, ignoring the courtyard. "She's been sitting in high chairs now. I have a soft cover in my bag I can place over top of the wood. It helps secure her and also keeps a barrier in between her and any germs left from other kids."

"Nonsense," Marcheline replied. "I enjoy holding her.

But maybe we will sit her in the highchair when our food comes. Is she eating any solids yet?"

"Nothing but breastmilk until the six-month mark," Sabine explained. "But we're getting close to it. She's interested in food, that's for sure. She's started watching us like a little hawk while Ryan and I take bites."

Marcheline was proud of what a good mom her daughter was. "I remember that phase from when you were a baby, Sabine. I breast-fed you, too. I remember reading books about attachment parenting by Dr. Sears and trying to do the very best for you I could. I didn't have anyone around to guide me."

Sabine smiled. "And then you taught me everything you know."

"I'd like to think I learned a little something along the way," Marcheline added, proud of herself. Amelie looked up at her and cooed.

"That brings me to what I want to talk about today," Sabine began. "Because I'd like to know more about our family history. And I don't just mean my father. I want to know more about your side of the family, too."

Marcheline sighed heavily. "This, again?"

"I'm sure you can understand my feelings if you try, Mom. Now that I have a daughter of my own, I want to know where she came from. Ryan's side of the family is so out in the open that I can just ask if we don't already know the answers to our questions. But my side of the family is all mysterious, and I don't think it should be that way."

Marcheline recoiled. She hunched her shoulders down and sat back in the booth. She didn't want to hear any of this. "I've told you," she said. "It is what it is, and I don't want to talk about it. Please, let it rest, Sabine. I beg you."

Sabine frowned, then tried to adjust her approach. "Mom, I'm not attacking you. Please don't take it that way. I'm just… Curious. Like with the thing about breast-feeding and six-month-old babies beginning solid foods. I wonder if your mother breast-fed you. And I wonder how early you started eating solids. Or what your first foods were. I'd like to know the same about my father."

"Sabine, don't."

When Marcheline had fled her dangerous circumstances as a young woman, she had cut contact with her parents, Jean-Claude and Francine Bisset. She hadn't seen or spoken to them since that cold November night when she was just nineteen years old, a full twenty-six years prior.

She had stopped at a payphone on her way out of town and called her parents to tell them she was leaving Chester and the state of Illinois. She hadn't even told them she was pregnant. She could still hear her mom's voice on the other end of the line, her heart breaking in real time. Marcheline didn't feel she could adequately explain. She thought her mother would never understand. Marcheline was running away and changing her identity to save herself and Sabine. It wasn't out of spite or malice. She hadn't wanted to hurt her parents. At that tender young age she hadn't even grasped the damage she was doing by running away. But she knew her decision was about survival. Leaving was the only way out she could see. And she knew she and Sabine deserved better than what her their future would have held if she had stayed.

"Mom," Sabine said, as gently as she could manage. "There are medical questions our pediatrician asks. Questions about diseases that run on my side of the family. Not to mention, my own doctor asks me the same. From what I understand, it will become even more important to know my medical history as I get older. Do you ever think of that? Do you consider what it's like for me to be kept in the dark?"

Sabine paused while the waiter arrived then introduced himself and placed two glasses of water on the table. He promised to return shortly to take their order.

Marcheline tried changing the subject without answering her daughter's questions. "Come now, dear," she urged. "Let's look at the menu so we can place our orders when the gentleman returns. I have only an hour right now. When that time is up, I will need to get back to the office for a staff meeting."

"Mom!" Sabine exclaimed, exasperated. "We've been to this cafe hundreds of times. You know what's on the menu. Will you stop avoiding my questions, please?"

"Sabine!" Marcheline returned, waving an open hand across the table at her daughter. "Darling, I know you have a lot of free time to ruminate on this since you're a stay-at-home mom now. But I'm busy, and I don't want to spend the time we have together in disagreement."

"Really?" Sabine muttered. "You're going to use work as an excuse for this, too? Unbelievable."

Marcheline had a hard time facing her past. She sometimes missed her parents terribly. She often had the urge to pick up the phone and call her mom. Even now, she would have liked Francine's advice on how to handle her daughter's incessant curiosity and probing questions. But Marcheline had been so terrorized by what had happened to her and the danger was so real, she couldn't risk being found. Not even by her own parents.

The waiter returned and took their order while Marcheline and Sabine smiled as if nothing was wrong. Marcheline chose a turkey club sandwich and a bowl of pumpkin soup. Sabine picked a chicken salad sandwich and a side salad. The food was usually served quickly at Brick House Cafe, so Marcheline estimated she only had to get through about ten more minutes until they would have their mouths full.

"Sabine, my dear girl," Marcheline said, looking her daughter in the eye. She had always thought Sabine's rich, brown eyes were one of her best features. "I love you more than anything in this world. And now I love Ryan and little Amelie the same. Do you believe me when I say this?"

"Yeah," Sabine said reluctantly, pouting. "So?"

"So, I need you to believe me when I tell you I have very good reasons for keeping some things from you. I've done it to keep you safe. Do you understand?"

"But, Mom," Sabine replied. "I'm a grown woman with a husband and baby of my own. I can handle more than you think."

"I know you're a strong woman," Marcheline confirmed. "My concerns aren't about you being able to handle the information. I'm telling you. It's dangerous. Too dangerous."

Sabine looked out the window into the courtyard and shook her head in frustration. Then she turned back to her mother, leaning forward with her elbows on the table. "Mom, come on," she began. "How about you believe me? This is more than just idle curiosity."

Marcheline's pulse raced. "Is something wrong? Is it Amelie?"

"Maybe I don't feel like sharing that information with you," Sabine said, an edge to her voice. "Maybe it's for your own good that you don't know."

"Mercy, Sabine," Marcheline said, growing angry now. "That's not fair. If something is wrong, I need you to tell me right now, young lady." She looked down at Amelie. The child appeared to be healthy and developing normally.

"Oh?" Sabine replied. "So you don't like it when the tables are turned? Funny how that works."

Marcheline fumed at her daughter's flippant attitude. She wondered what she could say to make Sabine understand, short of the truth. Because telling her the truth wasn't an option right now.

"It's not the same. I grew up and found myself in a completely different situation than anything you've ever known. Then I got us out. You and me. To save us. My past holds real danger, Sabine. I keep it from you to protect you and your family. But there's no reason for you to keep things from me. I've been a good mom to you. I don't deserve to be treated this way."

"Yeah, well, I think it is the same," Sabine replied. "I've been a good daughter to you. And there's nothing you could tell me at this point in time that Ryan and I couldn't handle." She leaned further forward towards her mom. "Are you afraid? Is that it? Are you sure it isn't you who needs protected instead of me?"

A tear formed in Marcheline's eye as she considered her daughter's question. She *was* afraid. She knew it. She had lived with her fear for many years. Not only that, it hurt her to quarrel with her daughter. They had always been close and had gotten along well. Marcheline didn't want this issue to put a wedge between them, especially now that baby Amelie was in the picture.

"If I told you, we'd all need protected. We're safe the way I have things set up. But if you go upsetting that equilibrium, I don't know what we will do."

At her wit's end, Sabine stood up and took little Amelie out of Marcheline's arms. "I just lost my appetite. Let me know when you're ready to have a serious discussion, adult to adult. Until then, I'll see what I can find out on my own."

Then Sabine left the cafe and left Marcheline alone, without even eating her sandwich.

3

Marcheline asked for the food to go, deciding to take Sabine's sandwich back for Rande. She silently cursed Chester Loor and everyone else involved who had forced her to flee and start a new life. Things would have been so much easier if she could have stayed home in Evanston, able to enter adulthood with the support of her parents and childhood friends. Although on the other hand, Marcheline would have missed out on some glorious aspects of current life. Her thoughts on the topic were a mishmash of gratitude and regret.

As Marcheline climbed into her Land Rover and set out on the drive back to Maison du Vin, she let herself imagine how things might have been.

Illinois was different from Northern California, to put it mildly. But Marcheline could have seen herself attending college there, just as she'd done out West. There were plenty of good universities in the Chicagoland area, and she could have seen herself studying business at any of them. She seemed to have a natural aptitude for the field. But Marcheline knew she wouldn't have landed at a winery if she'd graduated from college in Illinois. Grapes just aren't grown in that region. Maybe she would have opened a brewery instead. Or a restaurant. Or even a bakery, like her parents. She wondered if she would have gone on to the same level of success that she had with Maison du Vin. Much of her business' growth had been bolstered by the strong tourism industry in the wine country region. Tourists came to Chicago, of course, but it wasn't the same. Rosemary Run was a coveted spot for high-end travelers who wanted to spend a lot of money. And Marcheline knew how to wow them. In addition, she had an affinity for wine and for the aesthetic of the rolling hills of a vineyard. She had always thought there was something refined and elegant about the setting, and it suited her. Considering where she'd come from and all she'd been through, Marcheline wore her current elegant lifestyle as a badge of honor. She liked to think it harkened back to her Parisian roots.

If she were in Evanston right now, she would have been cold. The city often saw its first snow this time of year. If Marcheline lived there, she'd be bundled up in winter clothes, complete with a scarf wrapped around her neck and pulled up to shield her nose and mouth from the aggressive cold. It was a very different climate from the one she enjoyed in Rosemary Run. But each climate had its benefits. Snow had been a lot of fun to experience as a kid. Marcheline would have liked for Sabine to share that experience. The only time Sabine had seen real snow had been on trips to the Sierra Nevada Mountains. It was an entirely different thing to have snow fall on your own roof and your own front stoop then it was to take a trip to see it. And Marcheline wished the same for little Amelie. The thought of that baby girl bundled up in a warm Halloween costume was almost too much cuteness to handle. Add Oktoberfest along the shores of Lake Michigan plus brilliant leaves forced down by the first winter wind of the year and the thought made Marcheline downright homesick.

She wondered what her parents would say if she ever showed up on their doorstep a quarter of a century later. Would they be angry and slam the door in her face? Would her mother fall apart and drop to the floor in tears? Her mom and dad were both still alive. Marcheline knew because she had searched the Internet for them from time to time. Although, she felt badly every time she did, knowing that they couldn't do the same to find out about her. Her parents had no way to know that she was safe, or even still alive. Marcheline knew it must have been a terrible thing for them to face. She wasn't even sure what they thought had happened. As best she knew, her parents would have considered her missing. At least, they would not have had reason to presume her dead. They must have assumed she just ran away. Even though it was the truth, Marcheline hoped her parents might consider that there had been extenuating circumstances. She hoped they would have known their daughter well enough to realize she wouldn't make such a decision lightly.

Marcheline wished she could be as sure about personal matters as she was about business. Her lack of savvy in interpersonal relationships often embarrassed her. Her social development had been arrested in her teens.

Especially when it came to romantic relationships, Marcheline knew she was a mess.

Her relationship with Leonard was a prime example. He was a good man. He had a successful career and lived a balanced life. Leonard jogged every morning, kept his house clean, and was trustworthy and reliable to all who knew him. He had been too wrapped up in his career to marry or have children, but that didn't mean there was anything wrong with him. He was as good of a catch as any, and he understood what it was like to run a business that afforded him personal wealth. At least Marcheline knew he wasn't after her money, she reasoned. They were both at a point in their careers where they could slow down and branch out into personal pursuits they had previously been too busy to try. The two of them shared a lot of common interests, including hiking, French movies, and hot air balloon rides. On paper, they were a perfect match.

Marcheline and Leonard had been quietly dating for several months. She had been happy with their arrangement until recently, when Leonard decided he wanted more. Seemingly out of nowhere, he had told Marcheline he loved her and that he wanted them to move in together. He was tired of keeping such a low profile in her life and wanted to be front and center. He was ready to meet her family and for her to meet his. He had even mentioned the possibility of a wedding proposal in the not too distant future.

Marcheline realized that any healthy and functional woman in her position would have been thrilled with this natural progression. But she wasn't any healthy and functional woman. The very thought of what Leonard proposed made her go all weak and clammy. It was as if her body rejected his advances before her heart or mind had a say. She wasn't sure how she could ever move through the steps necessary for their relationship to move in the direction he wanted it to. Her trauma still had a grip on her, and it held her back.

As Marcheline pulled into her regular parking spot out front of the winery, she noticed a familiar vehicle next to her in the lot. She got out, carrying the sandwiches, and she walked around the back of the familiar vehicle. Sure enough, it was Jim Bennett's red Jeep Wrangler. The top was off and his favorite sunglasses were sprawled out on the dash. Marcheline had discouraged both Jim and Leonard from visiting her at work, mostly because they could bump into each other. Neither man knew about the other. She hadn't professed her devotion to either, and she hadn't promised exclusivity. But she knew it would hurt feelings if Jim or Leonard were to find out she was seeing someone else.

Hesitantly, Marcheline walked inside, past the reception desk towards her office. She didn't see Jim waiting in the chairs out front, so she knew someone must have shown him to a more private space. She pulled her smart phone out of her pocket to text Rande, hoping to avoid an awkward situation. But before she could, Rande stepped out of the conference room door, closing it snuggly behind him.

"Welcome back, Ma'am," he said in his characteristic drawl. "You have a visitor."

"Shush," Marcheline implored, pulling her friend to the side. "We need not make a spectacle."

Rande didn't reply, but he raised his eyebrows as his mouth moved into a smirk. He was enjoying this.

"Fine. We'll pretend there isn't a young, blonde high school teacher waiting for you in the conference room. Just be glad I didn't take him into your office where he could gawk at all your stuff," Rande explained. "Hey, did you bring something back for me?"

"Leave it to you to move right past my distress and onto the topic of lunch," Marcheline said with a grin.

"That's right," Rande replied. "I have my priorities straight."

Marcheline handed one bag to Rande, still smiling. Their friendship always boosted her spirits. "Chicken salad. It was supposed to have been Sabine's, but she saw herself out before the food arrived at the table. Figured I might as well bring it back for you rather than let it go to waste."

"My good fortune," Rande said. "You know I'd never let a sandwich to go to waste. Sabine's loss is my gain. I'll take it." Rande winked, then took the sandwich back to his office, leaving Marcheline to tend to Jim Bennett.

4

M archeline opened the door of the conference
room slowly, leaning only her head inside. There
was Jim, fiddling with this smartphone. He was probably
playing some juvenile game. He hadn't progressed all the
way through the teenage stages of development, as far as
Marcheline could tell. Perhaps that was why he related so
well to his students. And perhaps that's why the two of
them were attracted to each other. Marcheline had read
enough self-help articles to know that people from
dysfunctional childhoods often paired up. Misery loves
company.

Jim was wearing casual clothes. Even more casual than
he normally wore to teach at school.

"Hello, Mr. Bennett," Marcheline said softly. A broad
smile spread across Jim's face as he laid eyes on her.
"Come on. Follow me," she instructed.

"On it," Jim replied. He stood up eagerly and trotted
along behind Marcheline as if she were a mama duck.

Marcheline hated to feel embarrassed of Jim's age and

immaturity, but she did. They had a lot of fun together. But Jim wasn't who Marcheline thought she was supposed to be dating. He was in his late twenties, much closer to her daughter's age than her own.

Once they were both in Marcheline's office and the door was closed, she set the carry-out bag on her desk and turned to face Jim.

"What are you doing here?"

"I wanted to see you. Why else would I be here?"

His attention made Marcheline pause. She wasn't comfortable when a romantic partner lavished praise on her.

"I'm glad," she replied. "But I thought we said you weren't going to come to my office. I like to keep my personal life separate from my work life."

Jim took a step towards her. "You and Rande hang out together all the time."

"That's different. Rande and I are friends."

Jim took another step towards Marcheline playfully, reaching one arm around her waist. "But we're friends, aren't we?"

"Stop, now," Marcheline said feebly, feigning resistance.

"I mean it. We're very good friends, I might add," Jim said as he pressed his body up against Marcheline's. She could feel his breath. Jim had the muscles of a surfer dude, that was for sure. Being so close to him made Marcheline aroused.

"Come away with me," Jim whispered, the words dancing around her ear.

"What are you even talking about?" Marcheline asked,

leaning her arms against his chest. It was a defensive pose, but one that left open the possibility of relaxing her guard.

"Come away with me," he repeated. "East Valley High is on fall break this week. My schedule is wide open until next Monday. Come away with me."

Marcheline lowered her eyebrows, assessing Jim's face to see if he was serious. It was a preposterous idea. She had a winery to run. She rarely took time off, let alone to go on vacation. And besides, they had barely been seen in public together. They weren't officially dating, no more than she and Leonard were. Still, his offer was tempting.

"Think about it, will you?" Jim asked. "Just the two of us without obligations or responsibilities, cruising down the open road. We could head west to the ocean. Maybe spend a week at a little bungalow by the beach?"

"Let me guess," Marcheline said. "You surf?"

"Not a lot, but yeah, I do," Jim replied. "Why? You want to learn?"

"I don't know about that," Marcheline said. "This old girl might be too old for new tricks like surfing."

"Nonsense," Jim said as he pulled Marcheline more tightly against him. "First of all, you're not old."

"Older than you. You know I could be your mama. Doesn't that ever bother you?"

"Not in the least. I don't know any mamas as hot as you. Have you seen yourself? You're gorgeous."

Marcheline swooned. She was trying to resist, but Jim's charms were working. "I'm serious," she added. "I can't just get away like that. Especially without notice. If I were to go out of town, it would take me a couple of weeks of prep just to make sure everything was done properly in my absence. I've worked too long and too hard to be careless with my business. You're a doll, Jim, but I don't think you understand my level of responsibility."

Marcheline bristled at her own words. She immediately wished she could take them back, because she heard how condescending they sounded. Jim didn't seem fazed.

"Okay," he said. "Let's problem solve. Come on, I'll help you think through it. Can't Rande step up and fill in? He's worked with you for a long time now and seems very capable. Oh, I know! You could hire somebody from a temp agency to help Rande out. That way, the workload wouldn't be so heavy on him."

Marcheline appreciated Jim's enthusiasm, but he was beginning to irritate her. He had no idea what running a successful business was like. It was presumptuous of him to think he could begin to advise her on how to handle hers. He was just a high school teacher. He was way out of his depth.

Adding force to her arms, which were still positioned in between the two of them, Marcheline pushed Jim away. "This has been lovely, Jim, but I really need to get back to work," she said as she walked over and sat down behind her desk. "Thank you for the invitation, but I won't be able to go away with you at this time."

Jim looked at the floor, disappointed. He shook his head slowly. "You know you have a problem, right?" he asked. Marcheline clammed up, barely holding eye contact. "You're so scared of a real relationship that you're willing to push a good one away when it's right in front of you. Have you ever even been in love? You talk about how young I am like it's a bad thing, but I have. I know what love is. I'm trying to *show* it to you."

Marcheline crossed her arms over her chest in another defensive pose. She didn't want to hear this any more than she wanted to hear Sabine's talk about her perceived inadequacies. "That will be all, Jim. Thank you."

He took a breath, quickly realizing he would not get anywhere with Marcheline if he kept this up. He liked her. He didn't want to push her away. And he didn't want to offend her.

Without saying a word, Jim walked behind Marcheline's chair and placed his hands on her shoulders. He began to rub her shoulders and neck, kneading skillfully to release the kinks where tension was stored. Marcheline half-heartedly tried to resist, but was so wound up that her body wanted the release. She knew she needed to relax, and Jim's touch was just the thing to help her do exactly that.

"That's the spot," Marcheline mumbled.

Jim let his hands wander around the front to Marcheline's collarbone, then he slid his hands inside her blouse and over her ample bosom.

"I know a few other spots I can touch that might help you relax," he whispered as Marcheline arched her back in response.

"Are you trying to seduce me?" she breathed.

"I don't know. Is it working?" Jim asked as he let one hand travel all the way down below the waistline of Marcheline's pants.

Wrapped up in the heat of the moment, Marcheline stood quickly then pushed a button to close the shades on her picture window. She glanced at her office door to double check that it was locked. Satisfied they wouldn't be interrupted, Marcheline unbuttoned her blouse and pressed herself hard against Jim, kissing him deeply as he removed her silky pants and lifted her onto the desk in front of him.

His bodily response to her exposed skin was immediate, and Marcheline appreciated the vigor and vitality of a younger man. They fumbled with buttons and zippers, mouthing each other hungrily, until they both reached a climax, moaning with relief

5

"Whoa. That was hot," Jim remarked, sounding more and more like a surfer dude all the time. He moved through the process of zipping and buttoning in reverse as he pieced his clothing back together. "I think I get the message. Less talking and planning, and more of that."

Marcheline sighed as she buttoned her own blouse, careful to tuck everything back in like it was. "It isn't that simple."

"Maybe you could enlighten me. Over dinner tonight?" Jim asked. He knew they hadn't been seen in public together, but he was hopeful.

"I don't know," Marcheline said. "I have a lot left to do here. I went to lunch with my daughter, and now this. I'm behind on some things, including an afternoon staff meeting I need to lead. It's harvest season, you know."

"I'll get out of your hair," Jim replied.

"Thank you for understanding."

"How about this?" he tried. "I'll eat something now so

I won't be hungry early this evening. I'll wait on you in case we can steal away for a late bite."

"I…"

"Right," Jim added. "No stealing away because that means going out in public. I get it."

"I don't mean to hurt your feelings," Marcheline clarified. "I'm just… Well, I'm not really available. I'm sort of married to my business. I know that sounds bad to say, but it's just how it is."

"I get it."

"So, if we are to keep seeing each other…"

"We have to do it in private and around your work schedule."

Marcheline felt guilty for not being more available. Jim was a genuinely decent guy. So what if he was young enough to be her son? He liked her, and she liked him.

"Listen," Jim began in a soothing voice. He stepped close to Marcheline and brushed a few wild strands of hair from her eyes, tucking them gently behind one ear. "I want to see you. I'll be patient. And I'll do it the way you want. I'll check with you later this evening. If you get finished here at a reasonable hour, I'll stop by your house. I can bring takeout. It'll be fun. Netflix and chill?"

Marcheline was hesitant. She didn't know what time she'd be finished, and she didn't want to lead Jim on. Perhaps it would have been better for them both if she let him down easy and cut things off. At least that way, he could find someone who would return his affection fully. Marcheline knew Jim wanted a wife and kids someday. Even if by some remote chance she decided to marry, she was nearing fifty and wouldn't be bearing any more children. She didn't want to hold Jim back from the natural order of things. It wouldn't be fair. He would, no doubt, make a great dad. Marcheline had heard him talk often about the high school kids in his classes. She could tell he had an ease around kids that not everyone does. It seemed almost imperative that he raise a few of his own. But Marcheline's body craved more of Jim's touch. He had such a youthful lust for her. His sexual attention made her feel good. It made her feel wanted in a context other than business. Just thinking about a repeat of their afternoon encounter piqued her interest and sent blood rushing to all the right places.

"Okay, fine. Netflix and chill," she confirmed. "I'll text you when I'm leaving here. Probably around seven. I'll wrap up as soon as I can."

"Yes!" Jim exclaimed, pumping a fist in the air. "It's a date." Marcheline opened her mouth to correct him, but he corrected himself before she could. "I mean… See you tonight."

6

There was a knock on Marcheline's office door just minutes after Jim left. She assumed it was him. Maybe he had forgotten something. "Come in," she called from a seated position at her desk. She felt warmed by their lovemaking and wouldn't have minded seeing Jim for a few more minutes. She'd tell him how she had to hurry and get back to work, but secretly, she would enjoy an excuse to spend more time with him.

"It's me, Ma'am," Rande called back.

"Oh," she said. "Only you, huh?"

"Oh, only me," Rande teased. "Happy to see you, too."

"Get in here," Marcheline replied as Rande stepped through the door.

"Did you enjoy your... Um, what should we call it? Meeting... With young Mr. Bennett?" he asked. "That boy looked all hot and bothered when he left here. What is he, twenty now? Soon you'll be able to drink together."

"Is that all you came here to say, old man?"

Marcheline asked her friend with a laugh. "Because I really need to get back to work. This place won't run itself."

"Yep. Pretty much," Rande replied as they both chuckled. "But you have a phone call. The guy has been holding for quite some time. Stacy referred it back to me since she knew you were... Shall we say, otherwise occupied."

"Couldn't she have taken a message?" Marcheline asked. "Isn't that why we have a receptionist, anyway?"

"She could have, but I see where she's coming from. This sounded important. It's a guy named Bill Henderson, calling from Chicago."

"Chicago?" Marcheline's breathing suddenly became shallow as she tried not to panic. There were any number of reasons that a man from Chicago could have been calling related to the business. But that didn't stop her from fearing the worst.

"Did he say what he wants? To place an order? Or arrange for event space?"

"No. I got on the line and told him he might hold a while, but he said he wanted to wait. I asked him what this was in regard to."

"And?"

"He wouldn't tell me a thing," Rande explained. "He insisted on speaking only to you."

7

"Hello. Marcheline Fay here," she said, putting the receiver in one hand and gripping the arm of her office chair tightly with the other.

"Yes, hi there," a deep male voice replied. "You said it's Marcheline Fay speaking?"

"That's right. What can I do for you?"

"Perfect. My name is Bill Henderson. I'm a private investigator based in Chicago and I'm working on a case. I'd like to ask you a few questions."

Acting on instinct, Marcheline jumped in her chair as if she'd been struck by lightning. She slammed the receiver down, disconnecting the call. She was in shock. She wrung her hands in her lap, unsure whether her legs would hold her if she tried to stand. It had been a lifetime ago since she had spoken to anyone in Chicago. She had purposely avoided the city and its inhabitants, for good reason. She couldn't risk anyone finding out who she really was.

Her phone rang again, causing a second jolt. She

shifted her gaze to it, mixed emotions moving through her body. By the third ring, anger had won out and taken over.

"Hello?" she said forcefully.

"Ms. Fay, it's Bill Henderson. From Chicago. I think we got disconnected a few minutes ago."

"We weren't disconnected," Marcheline said. "I hung up the phone."

"You did?"

"I don't know anything about Chicago and I don't much like being bothered at work," Marcheline explained. "You have two minutes, so make it quick. What do you want?"

"Okay, wow. I wasn't expecting…"

"Wasting time."

"Right. I was hired by the family of a man named Chester Loor. He's serving time in federal prison for a crime they don't think he committed. I'm trying to help clear his name."

Marcheline was speechless. She tried desperately to hold on to her anger even though its strength threatened to leave her. She again gripped the arm of her chair tightly. She focused all of her energy on that grip, hoping it might steady her.

"Are you still there?" Bill asked.

"You have one minute left," she managed.

"I'm calling you because Chester's father, Norman Loor, received a letter addressed to Chester at his house. It's signed by you. Or someone posing as you."

"I don't know what you're talking about," Marcheline snapped, even though she knew exactly what he was talking about.

Sabine. My God, what have you done, Sabine? And Norman. The old coot. He never could leave well enough alone.

"If you would allow me… Um, I'd like to ask you a few questions," Bill continued, talking as fast as he could.

"No."

"Wait! Don't hang up. Ms. Fay, if you won't answer my questions, I'll have no choice but to turn the letter over to the authorities."

Marcheline's face grew hot like fire and she felt as if the room was closing in on her. But she was determined not to crumble. She hadn't worked this long and hard for the life she had to let herself fall apart in the face of adversity.

"You do what you want. I didn't send the letter. And this doesn't concern me," she said boldly. Then she hung up the phone with a bang.

8

"Rande, I'm going out," Marcheline said as she blew by his office on her way to the front door, fishing through her bag for car keys as she walked. She didn't slow down enough to even hear her friend's response. "Hold my calls," she said to Stacy. "And don't give out my mobile phone number."

"I wouldn't…" Stacy began, the alarm evident in her voice. She didn't finish her sentence.

Stacy Shepard was a blonde, thirty-something sorority-girl type. She looked like she was made from the same mold as Jim. The two of them could pass for siblings. She was a nice lady and did good work for Maison du Vin, but she wasn't someone Marcheline wanted to confide in. She certainly wasn't a friend like Rande.

"But… The staff meeting…" she tried.

"If there's an emergency, Rande will handle it," Marcheline called as she made her way out the door. "I won't be back today."

With keys in hand, Marcheline sifted through her handbag, this time to find her smartphone. She felt clumsy, as if there was suddenly a disconnect between her hands and her brain. She remembered this feeling. It had been a long time, but it wasn't a feeling one could easily forget.

It took longer than it should have to locate the phone and get it unlocked. Marcheline found Sabine's number and initiated a call as she got into the driver's seat of her Land Rover.

No answer.

She fumbled with the phone some more as she put the car into gear and backed out of her parking space. She tried her daughter again.

Still, no answer.

This time she left a voicemail. "Sabine, it's Mom. I need to speak to you immediately. I'm coming to you. On my way."

Hot tears welled up in her eyes as she pushed the button to end the call. She wondered how her daughter could have been so foolish. Marcheline didn't have to guess how Bill Henderson had gotten his hands on her letter or what he now knew after reading its contents. Sabine had been the only other person with access to that letter. Not to mention, she had been the only person with reason to mail it.

Marcheline scolded herself for ever having written the letter in the first place. She had done so when Sabine was a baby. It had happened during her college years when she was a young, single mom trying hard to get her mind right. Marcheline had watched an Oprah Winfrey

Show episode where a life coach suggested that getting your feelings out and onto paper would help heal emotional wounds. Marcheline could still see the woman's face, looking wise and confident as she told Oprah and her worldwide viewing audience how much writing such a letter would help. She had sounded so sure. The woman had emphasized how the healing effect would happen by writing a letter to the person who had hurt you, even if you never gave the letter to that person. She said it was part of the forgiveness process to tell the person who had wronged you exactly how their actions made you feel.

Chester and Marcheline had hurt each other. She needed to both air her hurts and apologize for the ones she'd caused him.

Seeking relief and endeavoring to better herself, Marcheline had followed the woman's advice and written a letter to Chester. She had never intended to mail it. She'd sealed the envelope and written the address on the front, but hadn't been sure why she'd gone to the extra trouble. Maybe it had felt more real that way. Or maybe a part of her thought the letter would be found and mailed some day in the distant future when Marcheline was dead and gone. That might have been okay, depending on Sabine's circumstances.

As she sped down the road toward Sabine and Ryan's house, Marcheline's phone rang, its familiar chime bringing her back to the present moment. She looked at the display, relieved to see Sabine's name and smiling face.

"Sabine!" Marcheline said as the car connected to the vehicle's audio system.

"Mom, is everything okay? You sound weird. I'm not mad about lunch. We can talk about it some more."

"No," Marcheline replied. "Well, yes. I mean, no one is hurt or anything. Yet…"

"Yet?" Sabine asked, puzzled. "Mom?"

"Yes, yes. I'm here. I'll explain when I see you. I'm on my way to your house. Are you home?"

"I am. Me and Amelie. Ryan is at work. But you're kind of scaring me. Please tell me what's going on."

"I will when I get there," Marcheline reiterated. "I'll see you in a few minutes."

As soon as she ended the call with her daughter, another call came in. This time, it was Leonard. Seeing his name and smiling face on the display was usually a pleasant experience, but not today. Marcheline had little time or patience this afternoon for anything other than her conversation with Sabine. She needed to think things through and come up with a plan. But Leonard was perceptive. If Marcheline avoided him, he'd get the idea that something was wrong and come looking for her. She decided she might as well answer to avoid it becoming an issue.

"Leonard, my darling," Marcheline said, trying to sound as normal as possible. "How is your afternoon going?"

"It's going quite well, thank you," he replied. Marcheline thought his voice sounded like it belonged to a banker, although she couldn't say exactly what that meant. "I'm calling to check in. I wanted to see how your day has been so far."

"You're so good to me," she said. For a moment, the

thought of Leonard's loving care made her smile and forget about everything else that was happening. She was skilled at pushing things out of her mind. It was a proficiency she had honed after a lot of practice.

"Why wouldn't I be? You're my best girl."

"Such a doll you are," Marcheline said. "Things are fine. Pretty much a typical day at the office. I stepped out to have lunch with Sabine. Ended up bringing sandwiches back for me and Rande." She hated to lie.

"Sounds like there's a story there."

"Yeah, nothing too out of the ordinary," Marcheline explained. "Maybe a little attitude from my only child. It happens. I'll tell you about it next time we see each other."

"I hope that will be soon."

"Me, too," she replied. "I always enjoy your company."

"Are you working late tonight?"

"I'm not sure yet. As you know, it's harvest season. There's a lot to do."

"Take it easy there. It's important to pace yourself so you don't get burned out. I speak from experience," Leonard explained.

Marcheline liked how wise Leonard was, but she sometimes resented his advice. She didn't want to *need* a man, preferring instead to be self-reliant in every way.

"I know it," she replied. "I hear you. I've been down that road before myself and it isn't pretty. Don't you worry. I'll take care."

"Good then. We'll speak again soon."

Marcheline and Leonard said their goodbyes and ended their phone call just as Marcheline turned into

Sabine's neighborhood. She glanced in the rearview mirror and straightened her earring that had gotten twisted as she coasted across the final, familiar stretch of road to Sabine's red bungalow.

A white picket fence stood proudly out front at 16 Songbird Way, a tidy boundary to mark the edge of the property. Elaborate landscaping covered the entire front yard, including flowers in front of the fence and native grasses and shrubs close to the porch. Three stone stairs lead to the covered porch, and a wooden front door was adorned with a round autumn wreath to welcome guests. To complete the look and the homey vibe, a porch swing hung from a linked chain while soft pillows bearing pumpkin and acorn prints waited on each side of its wide, wooden slat seat. The house was a cozy and beautiful place to live.

Marcheline had purchased the home as a wedding gift for her daughter and new son-in-law when they married a few years prior. She had let Sabine pick it out with the help of a local realtor and then had taken care of the cash purchase and the paperwork to get the property in Sabine and Ryan's names. Marcheline was gratified having been able to do it, one of the best rewards for all the hard work she'd put in over the years. It was the kind of luxury that made her sacrifices all worthwhile.

As Marcheline pulled into the driveway, she placed her hand on the lever to open the door before she even had the vehicle in park. She was doing her best to remain calm, but she didn't want to waste any time. She left her handbag in the car. She didn't plan to be there for long.

She took her keys and phone with her as she knocked on the door and stepped inside.

"Sabine, my darling, I'm here!" she announced.

Marcheline didn't wait for her daughter to appear. She went directly back to Amelie's room, then pulled a bag out of her closet and began packing it with clothes and blankets. She went methodically over a list of necessities in her mind as she filled the bag, adding diapers, toys, and Amelie's little pillow. She wasn't sure when they'd be back. She wasn't sure if they'd be back.

"Mom!" Sabine exclaimed as she arrived in the doorway and saw what Marcheline was doing.

"Now you're really scaring me. Are you packing an overnight bag?"

"Yes," Marcheline confirmed. "We have to go right away. Pack a bag for yourself and meet me in the car."

"Are you insane?"

"I wish I were," Marcheline replied. "This is very real and I'm very serious. Pack a bag for yourself. We have to leave."

Sabine looked baffled as she worked to process the scene unfolding in front of her. "This is my home, Mom. I have a husband and a baby. This is my life. I will not leave it."

Marcheline walked over to her daughter and placed her hands firmly on her shoulders, giving her a gentle shake. "We're in danger. We must go. Right now."

"Mom…"

"Right now!" Marcheline yelled, louder than she had ever raised her voice around Sabine before.

Mother and daughter looked at each other hard and

long, until finally, Sabine saw the truth in her mother's eyes and became willing to cooperate.

"Ryan?"

"We will call him when we get on the road. Hurry!" Marcheline implored.

Together, they packed a bag for Sabine and a second bag for Amelie filled with first aid items, bottles, and a manual breast pump. When they were ready, they woke the baby from her nap and carried her to Marcheline's Land Rover. The moment her car seat was securely attached and the straps were buckled, Marcheline put the vehicle in reverse and sped away, Sabine looking longingly at her home as it faded away from view.

"Where are we going?" Sabine asked.

"We're leaving town," Marcheline replied. "And we will stay away until we know it's safe."

Sabine had enjoyed a normal life until now. The dramatic circumstance she found herself in seemed more like something out of a movie or a TV drama than real life. "What about Limbo?" she asked, speaking quietly. "Who will take care of him? You can't leave a dog alone for very long. And I don't see a bag here for you. Did you pack anything?"

"I haven't been to my house since I left for work this morning. I didn't know we would need to get away like this. But I have a bag of necessities."

Sabine nodded, seeing her mom's demeanor and realizing the seriousness of the situation.

"I'll ask Rande to get Limbo. We can't risk going back to the house. It will have to be okay."

"I hope so," Sabine replied.

Marcheline reached her hand over and placed it on her daughters. "Darling, call Ryan. Ask him if he wants us to pick him up. If he stays, he should be safe here. But once we go, we must destroy our phones. It won't be safe to contact him. And I don't know when we'll be back. Please, stress the urgency of the situation when you speak to him."

"That's an impossible predicament to put him in," Sabine replied. "You know how big his extended family is and how close they all are. And his work! He loves his work. He won't want to leave Rosemary Run."

"I am sorry," Marcheline said. "I know this is overwhelming. But you and I have to go. We don't have any choice in the matter. It's not safe for us here anymore. And it's probably not safe for little Amelie. We can't be too careful where she's concerned. Call Ryan and ask him what he wants to do."

Sabine began to cry as the weight of the situation settled down on her. "Mom," she began. "Does this have anything to do with...?"

Marcheline immediately understood. "Yes, Sabine, it does. The letter."

9

Ryan didn't answer. Sabine had tried him five separate times, but he wasn't picking up. She was getting frantic.

"Mom," she pleaded. "What if something has happened to him? We need to go to his office and make sure he's okay."

"Stay calm," Marcheline told her daughter. "Keep trying his number."

Wishing to give her son-in-law a little more time, Marcheline pulled her Land Rover behind a tree line on a country road, then got out to check on her go bag. She walked to the back of the vehicle and accessed a hidden compartment near the spare tire. Everything was there, exactly where she had placed it. She checked and double checked. There was cash, burner phones, some items to help disguise her appearance, and a new California license plate. She removed the old plate using a screwdriver from her tool bag, then replaced it with the new one that would help them slip away undetected.

She knew the drill. She had gone over it countless times in her mind. She had hoped this day would never come. But since it had, at least she was prepared.

Marcheline pulled a ball cap out from her bag and placed it snugly on her head, tucking her long hair up underneath. She then pulled out a pair of aviator sunglasses and put them on. They differed from her usual style. She knew she needed to cut her hair and dye it for a more permanent change to her look, but the hat and glasses would have to do for now. Marcheline wouldn't tell her daughter at this juncture, but Sabine would need to change her appearance as well.

"Get him yet?" Marcheline asked as she walked around to her daughter's side of the vehicle. Sabine began to cry big, fat tears.

"He's not answering his phone," she said. "He's probably in a meeting. But he could be tied up for all kinds of reasons. He doesn't always answer right away. I know he'll call back as soon as he's able. But Mom, I can't leave without my husband... Without Amelie's dad."

Marcheline placed one hand against the roof of her Land Rover as she thought about what to do. Ryan would understand, she reasoned. He would never want to jeopardize his wife and daughter's safety. But at the same time, he wouldn't want to be separated from them if he could help it.

"Okay," Marcheline said when she had made her decision. "We will go to Rande. I need to do that, anyway. He'll be able to get a message to Ryan."

"And I'll keep calling him!" Sabine added. "Maybe

he'll pick up with just a little more time. If he looks at his phone, he'll see all the missed calls from me and know it's important."

"Yes," Marcheline said. "I hope so, my darling. I really do."

Sabine hadn't mentioned Marcheline's disguised appearance. She had been too preoccupied to say anything. Maybe she hadn't noticed. Her sole focus was on her husband. Marcheline understood. Even though she had never experienced a relationship like Sabine and Ryan's, she saw what it meant to her daughter. Beyond that, she knew what it meant for Amelie. Marcheline understood the importance of growing up with a father. Her own father had a profound influence on her. It had been one of the greatest tragedies of Marcheline's life that Sabine hadn't enjoyed the same.

Climbing back into the driver's seat, Marcheline texted Rande and instructed him to meet at their designated spot. The two of them had planned for this contingency. Rande would know what to do. She put the car back in gear.

"Where are we going?" Sabine asked, glancing back to check on Amelie. So far, the baby was staying calm and quiet. She was still in that period after her nap where her needs were all met and she was happy to simply observe everything happening around her with wide eyes. "Are we going to Ryan's office? Because I think that's a good idea. I can run in and try to find him. It won't take me long. I've been to his building lots of times, and I know exactly where to go."

"No, that's too dangerous. They might look for us there."

"Look for us?" Sabine asked, baffled. "Mom, you've got to tell me what exactly is going on. I'm on board. I'm cooperating. But I deserve to know."

Still on the dirt road, Marcheline slowed the Land Rover down as she turned to her daughter. She looked her in the eye. "You're right, Sabine. I owe you an explanation. And I intend to give you one."

"It's about time," Sabine said.

"Here is my promise to you, my darling. By the time we go to sleep tonight, I will tell you what this is all about. You have my word. But first, we have to get somewhere safe. There's much to do. Please, sit quietly and do as I ask. All will be revealed soon enough."

Sabine shook her head and stared out the window blankly. It was a lot to process, Marcheline knew that. She thought perhaps she should have warned her daughter. Maybe she had made a mistake by keeping it from her. It was one thing to keep it from Sabine when she was a child, but perhaps Marcheline should have told her at least some of the story once she reached adulthood. Doing so would have made today much easier for Sabine to grapple with. Every thought Marcheline had about the situation seemed to have a flip side that was equally compelling. If she had told Sabine, for instance, that might have created a dread and anxiety that would have been worse than the shock the young woman was experiencing right now. It was a difficult situation no matter how it unfolded.

Before Sabine could answer, Rande replied to Marcheline's text confirming that he'd be there. He didn't ask questions. He knew what this meant. Rande was a good friend, like no other. Marcheline said a silent prayer of thanks for him. He would help her get through this. She just hoped that in doing so, he wouldn't put his own young family in danger.

10

B y the time Marcheline pulled up at the county's
waste management facility, Rande was already there
waiting for her. They got out of their cars at the recycling
station and walked side-by-side to a compactor, the sound
of which would prevent others from overhearing what
they were about to say. Rande had two bags filled with
glass bottles. He handed one to Marcheline, then they
stood, bottles in hand while the compactor ran behind
them, and began to discuss specifics.

"I like the hat and glasses, Ma'am," Rande said in his
usual jovial voice. It was a relief for Marcheline, who had
spent the past hour barely breathing.

"I'm glad," Marcheline replied. "But I must say, this
wasn't how I expected to spend my afternoon. Thanks for
being there for me, Rande. You're a good friend."

"Somebody has to look after you," he replied. "How is
Sabine taking it?"

"So far, not well. I don't blame her though. I promised
I would explain things before we go to sleep tonight."

"I think that's wise. She deserves an explanation. Where are you headed?"

"For now, I'll follow Plan A," Marcheline said. Rande knew exactly which destination she was talking about.

"You'll need to ditch that vehicle," he added. Marcheline nodded. "There's a truck stop in a little town called Kingman. It's south of Vegas on the way to Phoenix. It's out of your way, but was the closest I could get to your route. It won't cost you much extra time. Go inside the diner and ask for a man named Carl Lowery. I'll let him know to expect you. He'll have transportation ready."

"Thank you, Rande."

"You have enough cash?"

"I do. I'm good in that regard. I've been stashing bags of it for so long now that I might have gone overboard. I should have enough cash to live on for several years if we need to."

The two of them stood quietly as the impact of that statement sunk in.

"I brought the paperwork," Rande said. "Are you ready to sign it?"

"Ready as I'll ever be," Marcheline replied. "It breaks my heart. But I knew all along things might turn out this way."

Rande pulled the paperwork out of his bag and a pen out of his pocket. With a few quick scrolls, Marcheline signed ownership of Maison du Vin over to him.

"You know, Ma'am," he added. "This is just a formality. Just paper. That's your business and it always will be. You let me know when you're ready and I will sign it right back over to you. My word is my bond. You know that."

"I know, Rande. But I can't imagine coming back. It's just too big of a risk. Like when your house is on fire, you know. The first thing you do is you get your family out safe. Everything else is just material. You don't run back into the flames. I can begin with a new identity. I can build a new business. It may never be as big as Maison du Vin. I might never be as successful or as wealthy as I would have otherwise been. But as long as I get my family out safely, that's what matters."

"I hear you," Rande added. "You have your house keys?"

"Right here," Marcheline said as she reached into her pocket. She took the Land Rover key off the ring and handed the rest over to Rande, complete with her Maison du Vin wine-bottle key chain they'd made for promotional purposes not long after Rande joined her team. "I trust you'll take care of Limbo for me?"

"You know it. My girls will get a kick out of having a dog. They've been begging for one."

A tear formed in Marcheline's eye. She loved her dog. She'd even thought about taking him with her. Rande put his arm around his friend's shoulders.

"Forgive me," Marcheline said. "I'm trying to do this without getting emotional. But I love that old hound."

"I know you do, Ma'am," Rande added. "He'll be a guest in our home and we will treat him like family. But if you ever come back or if you want to send for him, he's your boy and I'll be sure he gets to you."

Marcheline sniffled. "Leave it to me to get choked up over the dog."

"You're a tough broad who is a softy at heart," Rande said with a chuckle.

Marcheline smiled back. "Ryan needs dealt with," she said, moving on. "I offered to pick him up and take him with us, but he isn't answering his phone. Sabine is freaked out. Can you get a message to him?"

"Of course," Rande replied. "What do you want me to say?"

"That's precarious, because I don't want to keep him from his wife and daughter. But people might be watching and listening, and we can't endanger them. Ryan wouldn't want that."

"I agree."

"Please, get word to him that we had to go away, and explain that it was life or death circumstances. Please impress upon him the need for discretion in this matter. Tell him just enough so he understands the gravity, but not too much. I don't want him and his extended family getting tangled up in our mess."

"Good thing I only know just enough," Rande said.

"Rande…" Marcheline replied, tilting her head to the side as she looked at him. "I would tell you, but…"

"I understand," he replied. "Don't give it another thought. It was just an offhand remark. I know you want to protect me and my family as well."

"I do. Absolutely, I do."

"Then I'll tell him just enough. How else can I help, Ma'am? You name it, and it's done."

"At this point, I don't know. I might reach out to you if

I can figure out anything else. Do you remember the code word?"

"I do. I'll await your signal," Rande confirmed. "Do you remember my code name, for when you meet with Carl?"

"I do."

"Good girl."

"Then I guess this is it," Marcheline said, choking back tears as her voice broke. "Time for a new name, a new look... A new city..."

"A new everything," Rande said, finishing her sentence for her. "Which means, a new lease on life. A new freedom. You did it once. You can do it again. And Sabine is stronger than you give her credit for. After all, she was raised by you, Ma'am. She's going to be okay."

"I hope so."

"What do you want me to tell that pair of boys?"

"Oh yeah," Marcheline said. "Is it bad that I almost forgot about the two of them?"

Rande laughed. "I guess it says a little something about the status of your relationships. But none of that matters now."

"Tell them what you want. Just be sure to emphasize that it wasn't them. You know the old cliché about how it's me, not you."

"That might work."

"It's funny," Marcheline added. "Jim wanted me to go away with him. On a road trip west to the beach. I told him I couldn't possibly leave the company because I had so much important stuff to do. And here I am... Going on a road trip, but not one of my choosing. Southeast. Life can sure be ironic at times."

"Agreed. I'll let them down easy. But that begs the question. What do you want me to tell people about where you went? If they think you're missing, police will come calling. They may fear you're in harm's way. We need some type of cover story to keep that from happening."

"Well, yeah," Marcheline replied. "We've talked about this before. Just pick an option. Whatever you think is best. Truly, Rande. I have so much to think about going forward. At this point, talk of my cover story and Rosemary Run feel like going backward."

"I've got it," he said, raising a finger. "I'll tell people you went off grid to care for an ailing relative. That should cover all the bases. That way they don't think something is wrong with you. And they'll understand the need for such a sabbatical. Hopefully, they will feel sympathetic towards you rather than angry that you left."

"Yes, that's good, Rande. You're good at all this lying and scheming. You sure you're not some kind of superspy in disguise?"

They laughed together some more. It felt good to break the tension.

An old black pickup truck pulled in beside the Land Rover and a man got out with his bags of recycling. Marcheline didn't want to be seen here with Rande, so she tilted her head down low as she threw her bag of glass bottles into the bin. Rande turned towards her, his back shielding her from the other man's view. Marcheline leaned hard against her friend's chest and they embraced each other, even though they kept their arms at their sides.

Rande was a true gift to Marcheline. She told herself that whenever she doubted her ability to have healthy relationships, she should think back to her friendship with Rande. What they had was real, and it was enduring. She only hoped they'd be able to reunite someday and continue their friendship in person.

"You take good care, Ma'am," he said as he leaned down and placed a gentle kiss on the top of Marcheline's head.

"You too, Rande, my darling. I'll be forever grateful to you for what you're doing. And for who you are. You're a gift to me. A gift in my life. I sure am going to miss you."

With that, Marcheline walked back to the Land Rover, climbed in, and drove away.

11

M archeline drove south out of town with her daughter and granddaughter in tow. Sabine had protested when Marcheline destroyed both of their phones and threw them out in a gas station trash can on the outskirts of Rosemary Run, but she was coping. Marcheline wasn't sure whether it was a case of shock or a display of strength, but it was encouraging.

The trio was heading for Tucson, Arizona, not far from the US-Mexico border. Marcheline had a friend from college who was a Mexican national. They had dated briefly, and during their time together Marcheline had told Guillermo Martinez a portion of her story. He had promised on the spot to provide safe haven for her if she ever needed it, regardless of how many years in the future her need came to pass. He had grown up in Tucson, but had family across the border just sixty miles away in Nogales, Sonora, Mexico. Guillermo guaranteed he could keep Marcheline hidden in both places.

She hadn't done it often, because she didn't want to

leave any trace of who she was communicating with. But every once in a while, Marcheline had driven out of town and gone into a public library where she could search for Guillermo and keep tabs on his whereabouts without being detected. The last she had seen, he was a professor of Computer Science at the University of Arizona in Tucson. Marcheline knew she could count on his help. She didn't plan to alert him that she was on her way, out of an abundance of caution. She knew that when she showed up on his door, he would take her, Sabine, and Amelie in until they could find more permanent living quarters.

Marcheline kept moving, making her way several hundred miles south on I-5 before getting something to eat. She wanted to reach Kingman before stopping for the night because she was eager to switch vehicles. It was almost a ten-hour drive from Rosemary Run, not counting stops. She wasn't sure what kind of hours Carl kept, but she wanted to make herself available to him just as soon as humanly possible. The slightest delay could make all the difference in whether they were able to get away safely.

Sabine kept Amelie entertained so they could stay on the road, climbing in the backseat to nurse her and change her diaper right in her car seat. For her part, Amelie was a perfect sweetheart. It was almost as if she knew how important it was that they get away and keep moving.

"Mom?" Sabine began, as she climbed back into the front seat after a feeding session. "I've waited patiently for hours now. It's time for some answers. Do I need to remind you just how much this is costing me?"

Marcheline started to put her daughter off, as that was

her habit. She had become good at avoiding difficult topics and dodging uncomfortable conversations. But she knew Sabine deserved better.

"Fine," Marcheline said. "We'll talk while we drive. We have hours left to go and we might as well do something to pass the time."

"Finally!" Sabine exclaimed. "Thank you. Now, what in the hell is going on?"

"That's a big question with a complicated answer," Marcheline replied. "But I'll do my best to start at the beginning."

"At the beginning, meaning with who my father is?" Sabine tried. "I've been asking that question damn near all my life. I would love an answer. Would absolutely love it."

"My darling, it's complicated." Marcheline took a few deep breaths to steady herself before continuing. She wanted to be strong and hated to admit it, but talk of Sabine's conception made her feel like a vulnerable nineteen-year-old girl all over again. It made her feel helpless and alone, her parents too buried in work and oblivious to what their daughter was going through. "The first thing I'm going to tell you may come as a shock. Try to prepare yourself."

"Okay…" Sabine replied. "I'm not sure how much more of a shock I could receive at this point."

"More shock is always possible, believe me," Marcheline said.

"Okay. Well?"

"There's no easy way to say this, so I'm just going to come right out and do it." Marcheline looked straight ahead as she spoke, afraid to make eye contact. "My real name is not Marcheline Fay."

"What? You must be kidding."

"Unfortunately, I'm not," Marcheline replied. "My real name is Leena. And I have parents. We are from Paris."

"You mean your parents are still alive?"

"Yes, they are," Marcheline confirmed. "At least, as far as I know. I try to search for them on the Internet from time to time. As far as I can tell, they're alive and well in Evanston, Illinois, a suburb just north of Chicago where I grew up."

"And you haven't had contact with them?"

"Not since the day I left, twenty-six years ago."

Sabine was silent for a moment as she tried to process the information. "That means my last name isn't really Fay. And here I thought I was keeping my name when I married Ryan and didn't take his. That was all a crock of shit. All those hours debating about keeping my identity intact and what that would mean as an example for Amelie. And here my last name isn't even my own last name. How could you let me go through that?"

"I had to change my identity to keep us safe," Marcheline insisted. "I swear, Sabine. I didn't have any other choice. But I took great care in choosing your name. Sabine is after a great-aunt back in Paris who was very special to me. We left Paris when I was a toddler, but I still have memories of Aunt Sabine. I named you after her. And Fay, well it was my paternal grandmother's maiden name. I figured it was far enough in the distant past that no one would connect us. But it still allowed me to hold on to a tie to our roots. Please, go easy on me. I gave you the very best name that I could under the circumstances. It's one that meant a great deal to me."

"Maybe I could manage to go easy on you if you'd tell me what made you do it," Sabine asked. Her voice was faltering. She seemed to teeter between compassion and anger.

"My darling," Marcheline began again. "It's okay to be angry at me. I would be, too, if I were in your position. I'm angry at myself. I'm angry at the situation. It's all very sad and frustrating. I just ask that you be respectful and try to consider my position. To consider what I went through."

"Okay, tell me about it," Sabine prompted.

"I never wanted to leave my parents. They were good to me and like I said, I loved them very much. They worked a lot because they owned a French bakery in town and it took up most of their time. But I knew they were doing it for me. They wanted me to have a better life. The same as I wanted for you. Times were tough back in Paris. There was little money to go around and we lived in a small flat without room to stretch. When we came to America, we had a house with a yard. I had a good school to attend. And we had enough money to be comfortable with financial security. That was something my parents didn't think they could ever achieve back home."

"If it was that good and you were close to your parents, how could you leave them? Where do they think you went? You just... Disappeared?"

"I called them from a payphone the night I was leaving and I told him I had to go away. I let them know that I loved them, but that I didn't have a choice. I'm sure they were heartbroken, same as me. But at least they know I chose to go. I hope they know that they raised me well enough that I could take care of myself. They're the ones who instilled a strong work ethic in me. It's because of Mom and Dad that I've been able to build Maison du Vin into what it is today. Even as a young woman, it was because of Mom and Dad that I was able to complete college with good grades, all while being a single mother. If I'd been raised by different parents, I might not have had the fortitude."

Marcheline gripped the steering wheel tightly as she drove and talked.

"What were their names?" Sabine asked. "What is our real last name?"

"Sabine, I hope it goes without saying, but once I tell you this information, and once I tell you these names, you can't repeat them to anyone. You can't even communicate them to Ryan until we're sure he's not being followed or monitored. I mean it. This is *life and death*. What I'm about to tell you doesn't leave the confines of this vehicle until I say so, and then it's only to be shared with Ryan. Do you understand?"

"I understand."

"My last name is Bisset. My parents are Jean-Claude and Francine Bisset."

"Wow," Sabine replied. "Sabine Bisset. I'm not sure what I was expecting. This day feels foreign and strange. I've always liked Fay. But I like the idea of having a real name with more tangible roots. I've longed for grandparents. You have no idea how much. I didn't want to hurt your feelings because I've always known you did the best you could for me, but it means so much to know that I actually have more family out there."

"I can imagine," Marcheline added. "I never wanted to deprive you of that. It's made me sad every day."

"Do you have brothers or sisters? Do I have aunts or uncles? Oh! And cousins? Does Amelie have cousins? Do I?"

"No, I don't have any siblings. My parents moved over from France when I was young and I think they were too busy building their business to think about giving me a brother or sister. Sometimes I wished for a playmate when I was young. But it was all I knew and so I didn't spend much time back then thinking about how it might have been different." Marcheline continued to grip the steering wheel. She knew the hard questions were yet to come. "As for you, no living siblings. You know that. If I had a child out there, I'd move heaven and earth to keep them with me. The same as I did for you. The same as I'm doing for you right this very moment."

"I believe you, Mom," Sabine confirmed. "You're a good mom to me. Please don't ever doubt that." Sabine reached up and placed one hand gently on her mother's shoulder, then let it rest there. "Go on."

"The rest of the story gets harder to tell," Marcheline explained. "It's an ugly part of my history that I don't like to think about, much less talk about."

"Mom, it's okay. Go on. I can handle it. And besides, I'm here to support you. I'll help you through whatever it is we have to face together."

"Oh, my darling, those words are music to my ears,"

Marcheline confirmed. "I appreciate them." She took a
deep breath. "Okay, so, I was a lonely teenager who felt
out of place. My dark skin, curly hair, and French accent
weren't the norm in Evanston. They certainly weren't the
norm at my school, which was comprised of affluent kids
who were mostly white. With my parents at work so
much, I grew restless. A lot happened, but I ended up
getting involved with a boy named Chester who lived
across the city line. He lived in a rough part of town and
was involved in some shady things. He was
fundamentally a good guy, but he wasn't able to escape
the perils of the low-income, crime infested
neighborhood that surrounded him. Mom told me never
to associate with anyone like him, so doing so felt risky
and dangerous. I guess I wanted a little excitement in my
life. Either that or I wanted to numb my pain. I'm not
sure which motivation was the one that compelled me.
Maybe both. I started hanging out with Chester after
school when my parents didn't know. They thought I was
at home doing homework like a good little girl, but
instead, I was riding around in the passenger seat of
Chester's Cadillac, a car he had purchased with drug
money."

"Mom!" Sabine said. "I never would have pictured
that."

"Me neither," Marcheline said, somberly. "I took a
bad turn, to put it mildly."

"Is Chester the C.M. Loor the letter was addressed
to?"

"Yes," Marcheline confirmed. "How long ago did you
mail that letter, anyway?"

"It was one day last week," Sabine replied. "I don't remember exactly. Why? What's the big deal?"

"It's a huge deal. But ultimately, I take responsibility for writing the letter and for not destroying it. I wish you hadn't gone through my things. I *really* wish you hadn't mailed that letter without my permission. Who does that, Sabine?"

"I'm sorry, Mom. I really am. I was just so eager to find out about my father. I was looking through your things in the attic in the hopes of finding some evidence with his name on it. I'd asked you so many times and you refused to tell me anything, so I decided to take matters into my own hands, like I told you at lunch today."

"If we weren't in such a mess, I'd admire your determination," Marcheline said. "But yes, that's my Chester. His dad received the letter, and I got a call at my office this afternoon from a private investigator hired by the family."

"What?" Sabine asked. "Why does a private investigator need to get involved over a letter? What in the world did it say, Mom?"

"I never should have written it. I certainly never should have kept it. Maybe I could have written it and then burned it or something, I don't know. But I wrote it… To apologize."

"Because Chester is my father, and you took me away from him?"

"I wish it were that simple," Marcheline explained. "I swear, Sabine. I truly wish it were that simple."

"Mom!" Sabine exclaimed, exasperated. "Why is it like pulling teeth to get this story out of you? Won't you just tell me? Just, spit it out. What's the worst that can happen?"

"You have no idea."

Amelie cooed happily in the backseat as she chewed on a teething ring. The sun was setting over the mountains and they were getting hungry for more to eat.

"Why don't we continue this conversation after some dinner?" Marcheline asked. "I think it would be easier if my stomach weren't growling. How about we stop for fast food? We'll run in and out quickly, then eat in the car. It will be just enough time to stretch our legs, but hopefully, we won't be there long enough to be caught on camera."

"Unbelievable," Sabine muttered. Marcheline wondered why she had felt the need to use that word twice in one day. It seemed particularly cool and dismissive.

"Come on, my darling. We've got to eat," Marcheline said as she veered off an exit and peered forward over the steering wheel as she selected from the handful of fast food options. "What do you want? Chicken? Burgers?"

"I really don't care, Mom," Sabine replied begrudgingly. "You choose. Like you've done for me my entire life."

12

Back in Rosemary Run, Bill Henderson had arrived and set up camp at the Lazy Dayz Motel. It was a shady joint in an old area of town frequented by undesirables. Bill parked his red rental car out front, then went into his room and popped open in his laptop. He smoked a cigarette before getting down to business.

Now that he had Marcheline's name as a strong lead to go on, Bill knew the case would move along quickly. It had been nearly eighteen months since Norman Loor first hired him to find out if Chester had been wrongly convicted. A random lottery win from a scratch-off ticket had given Norman the means to pay for Bill's services, but the case had stalled not long after it started.

Things were finally going Bill's way. The letter sent by Marcheline in which she apologized for having falsely accused Chester was a break no one had seen coming. It would have been easy enough for Bill to take the letter straight to the police. He had long-time contacts on the force who would have opened an investigation and notified the Loor family's attorney. But Bill suspected there was more going on, and he didn't want to spill the beans until he had a complete picture. It was his job to find out everything there was to know. He intended to turn every stone. He took pride in doing so on every case he investigated.

As he stared at the blinking laptop screen, eager to get started now that he had set foot in town, Bill pulled out a notepad and pen from the desk drawer and begin making a list. First, he would go to Marcheline's house. Her address on Jenny Lane was printed plainly in an Internet directory. It had only taken him a few clicks to find it. He knew she would probably turn him away and refuse to answer questions, if she opened her door at all. But it was worth a try. Bill would look for anything unusual on her property, and he'd assess her lifestyle and present situation. Based on the search results about her online, it appeared Marcheline had a lot to lose. And he knew from experience that people who have a lot to lose often have things to hide.

Once he was finished scoping out Marcheline, Bill would move on to her closest family, friends, and associates. He'd learn about her from every angle, and would then use his instincts and experience to decide which avenues he should pursue most aggressively. He had already spoken to Marcheline at the winery along with her vice president, Rande. So, that was an obvious place for him to pursue further when they reopened in the morning. He Googled Rande and then read his bio and looked at his photo. The Maison du Vin website was thorough and made Bill feel like he already knew both Rande and Marcheline.

What piqued Bill's interest most of all was the fact that Marcheline appeared to have a daughter. Sabine Fay was the only other person with that last name listed in the white pages as residing in Rosemary Run, California. Jackpot. If Chester Loor had a long lost daughter, Bill intended to find out about it.

13

B y the time Marcheline and Sabine got Amelie in and out of the fast-food restaurant, darkness had fallen. Exhaustion had set in from all the adrenaline that had been coursing through their veins. They ate their food as they continued south on the interstate, filling their bellies with chicken fingers, biscuits, and rice, then washing it down with soda. Normally, neither Sabine nor Marcheline would have consumed such low-quality junk food, but they were too far out of their element to be vigilant about their eating. Their worlds were turned upside down, and healthy food was the least of their worries on this particular day.

For reasons Marcheline didn't fully understand, Sabine stopped asking questions and instead balled up a sweatshirt and leaned her head on it to go to sleep. Amelie napped, too, so Marcheline drove in silence for hours that felt like days. Maybe Sabine had reached her limit for one day. Marcheline knew it would be especially hard for her daughter to go to bed tonight without Ryan. Being away from home would only make things worse. Marcheline figured the rest Sabine was getting would help her cope, so she let her daughter sleep while the car was moving. They traveled on, into the night, until finally arriving in Kingman, Arizona around midnight. The town was quiet as stars shined brightly overhead. Mountains in the distance gave it a cozy feel. Marcheline thought it might be a nice place to visit if she weren't running from trouble. There was a stillness that spoke to her. The air was cool and clear.

Marcheline located the truck stop Rande had described with no trouble. It was right off the exit and had a diner attached, exactly as he'd said. Both were open twenty-four hours. It looked like an older establishment, probably built several decades before and not remodeled since. The look had its charm. It reminded Marcheline of road trips with her parents taken when she was a kid. They had ventured to Wisconsin Dells several times each year, spending long weekends at a frontier-themed amusement park and stopping at truck stops along the way. She had never understood why her parents liked that vacation spot so well, although she guessed they'd had a fascination with the Wild West era of American history. Maybe they identified with the brave families who packed their belongings onto wagons and set out for a new life, much the same as they had done when they emigrated from Paris.

Marcheline parked the Land Rover, then woke Sabine and asked her to remain alert while she went inside to find Carl. Her steps were short and quick as she hurried inside, wrapping her arms tightly around her body to keep warm.

The clerk behind the counter seemed bored and unsatisfied as he stared blankly at the front door. He looked like he had seen little excitement that night. His eyes barely registered her presence when Marcheline opened the door and stepped inside.

"Hello," Marcheline said, her voice flat. She was nearly out of energy for the day. "I'm looking for a Carl Lowery. Is he here?"

"Huh?" the man asked, dumbly. He picked up a dusty beige phone and dialed three numbers. Marcheline couldn't see which numbers he had pressed, but she was suddenly filled with panic at the prospect of them being 9-1-1.

"Who are you calling?" she asked nervously.

After a pause, the man replied. "You want Carl, right?"

Marcheline looked him over more closely. His name tag read Stu. She was leery and not sure if she could trust him. "Stu, is it?"

"Yeah," the man said.

"Short for Stuart?"

"Yeah."

"Stu, darling, I've been traveling a long way and I'm very tired. If you don't mind, I'd appreciate your assistance finding Carl. If he isn't here, it's no problem. I'm happy to come back in the morning. I'll just find a motel room nearby and be back when the sun rises."

"Do you want me to call him or not?" Stu asked, the receiver still held against his ear. It was obvious to

Marcheline that he would not be a whole lot of help, but she knew better than to make an enemy out of him.

"I do want to reach Carl," Marcheline replied. "But I don't want to wake him. Are you calling him at home? Or... Who are you calling?"

"Hang on," Stu said in a disgruntled voice as he set the receiver down on the counter without hanging it up. He stood, then ambled around and walked into a back room.

Marcheline remained nervous with the phone off the hook and Stu out of sight. She had to be vigilant. For all she knew, he was summoning the authorities from a phone in the back that very moment, which might have been in addition to the 911 call just placed and still connected. She looked around quickly, scanning for security cameras. As she suspected, there were two in plain sight, pointed straight at her. Marcheline had to be very careful to not seem suspicious. She was wearing her hat, but it would have looked strange if she'd worn her aviator glasses this time of night. The hat provided some disguise, but not nearly enough. She *had* to act normal.

A clock on the wall ticked loudly as the seconds went by, each one feeling like an eternity. Marcheline tapped a finger in the inside of her pants pocket as a small release of her nervous energy. It was all she could do to hold herself together. She needed to keep traveling south to evade Bill Henderson and anyone else who might come looking for her. Remaining still this long made her vulnerable. She didn't like it.

When she couldn't stand it anymore, Marcheline picked up the receiver of the phone to listen in. She knew she'd be recorded on camera doing so, but decided it was worth finding out whether authorities were on the other end of the line. She placed the receiver to her ear, but heard nothing. The line was silent, apparently dead. Taking a breath of relief, she placed the receiver back on top of the phone where it belonged.

As she continued to wait for Stu, she glanced out at the Land Rover where Sabine and Amelie were. The vehicle was parked in the shadows, so she couldn't see what was happening inside, but the doors were closed and things seemed quiet. Only two other vehicles were nearby in the parking lot. One was pumping gas and the other was parked on the far side. A single, tall light shone from above, but it didn't cover the entire property. All things considered, Marcheline felt safe. At least, for the moment.

When Stu hadn't returned after five minutes, Marcheline decided to go into the back and find out what he was doing. She walked around the counter, past the coolers that held sodas and beer, and she opened a door with a long, silver latch. She thought it might have been locked, but the latch loosened and allowed her entry without resistance. When the door swung open, there was Stu, leaning against the wall and smoking a cigarette. He wasn't even holding a phone.

"Stu!" Marcheline exclaimed. "I thought you were finding Carl for me."

"I wasn't sure if you wanted me to or not, so I'm taking a smoke break," Stu said, clueless.

Marcheline wondered if Rande had known about this dimwit. She shook her head and sighed heavily. "Look, Stu," she tried. "Will Carl be here tomorrow morning?"

"Yeah. Usually. I think so," Stu mumbled.

"Fine," Marcheline said. "Tell Carl that a friend of Rande's will be here in the morning to see him. Can you do that? Can you remember? Rande is the name."

"Yeah, sure, lady," Stu said. He didn't sound convincing.

Marcheline was frustrated. She had been hoping to change vehicles and get back on the road before stopping for the night. It wasn't the end of the world to stay in a motel nearby. She had known it might go that way. But she wasn't nearly as comfortable as she would have been if they'd been able to travel a little further. She used the restroom in the truck stop and bought a few bottles of water with cash before heading back out to the vehicle to talk to Sabine about their next move.

When she returned to the vehicle, Sabine was wide awake and had Amelie on her lap in the passenger seat. The two of them were chatting away together, the baby seemingly unfazed by the disruption to her usual routine.

"Well," Marcheline began. "I was supposed to meet a man here who will help us get a different vehicle, but he won't be in until the morning. The guy at the counter wasn't much help."

"Okay, wow," Sabine said. "I thought we were stopping here for the night, anyway. There's a hotel right next-door. I didn't know about the car thing."

"I guess this hotel is as good as any," Marcheline replied. "It doesn't have to be fancy. We just need a place to stay until morning when I can come back here and we can get the car. We will get back on the road after breakfast."

14

As the clock ticked past midnight at the red bungalow on Songbird Lane in Rosemary Run, Ryan Martin had been missing his wife and daughter. Rande Floyd had gotten a message to him to say they'd left town under life and death circumstances, but Ryan couldn't begin to imagine what those circumstances were. More importantly, he didn't intend to let his wife and daughter go quietly or without a fight. They were everything to him. Ryan was a fiercely devoted husband and father. He would find a way to get to them.

Ryan had been sitting on the couch in his living room, his hands clasped together with his elbows on his knees, staring at the stone fireplace as he'd thought about how to find his girls. He was mad at Marcheline for taking them away from him. He had wondered if she was out of her mind. None of it made sense. Why would a woman like Marcheline walk away from her mega-successful business after spending so many years building it through her own sweat and tears? Something wasn't right.

Ryan had considered calling the police. The local force in Rosemary Run had a good reputation for being thorough and diligent. But Rande had urged him not to do so. Further, Rande had explained that involving the authorities could actually endanger his wife and daughter. Left with little to go on, Ryan was becoming increasingly distraught.

Unexpectedly, his telephone had rung. It was the landline and not his mobile. He had known the moment he heard the tone that it was Sabine. No one else would have called so late at night, and hardly anyone uses the landline anymore.

"Sabine!" Ryan had said as he grabbed the receiver off the wall in the kitchen.

"I don't have long," Sabine replied. "Mom is in a truck stop right now and she'll be back any minute. I don't want her to know I'm calling."

"Understood."

"We're in a town called Kingman, Arizona. We're staying at a little motel called Desert Vista Inn. It's right next to the truck stop as soon as you get off the first Kingman exit. Don't tell anyone where you're going. I'll stall Mom until you arrive. She destroyed our phones, so you'll have to find us the old-fashioned way. We're in her Range Rover. Hurry!"

Ryan had hung up the phone, overjoyed. He had hesitated, ever so briefly, as he thought about his extended family. His parents, grandparents, brothers, and a slew of nieces and nephews were very special to him. They were a tight group, and he had chosen to spend his life living near them. But not if it meant giving up on Sabine and Amelie.

His extended family would understand. He had to go to his wife and daughter, even if it meant never returning to Rosemary Run.

Ryan had thrown a few clothes in a bag and then retrieved some important documents from the safe. Their birth certificates, marriage license, and their passports had been neatly organized and ready to grab at a time just like this. He had tossed the items in hastily, barely remembering to lock the house as he left. He had gotten into his black SUV and driven away as his tires squealed on the driveway.

Little had Ryan known; he was being followed. Bill Henderson had left the Lazy Dayz Motel to pursue his leads in person. When he had found no one home at Marcheline's estate on Jenny Lane, he had proceeded to the Fay-Martin residence on Songbird Lane. Bill hadn't planned to knock at this hour, but had been intrigued when he'd seen Ryan leave in a hurry. Deciding to chase the lead as far as he possibly could, Bill had followed discreetly behind Ryan, south towards Kingman, Arizona.

15

M archeline, Sabine, and Amelie got settled into the hotel room easily. They were traveling light and didn't have much to carry inside. Marcheline brought her go-bag in with her, wanting to keep the cash and other important items close by. She knew that if she were to lose anything from the bag, life on the run would become much more difficult.

Amelie continued to be a little angel. As long as she was fed, entertained, and given enough quiet to recharge, she rolled with the punches like a seasoned traveler. Amelie and Sabine took one bed, cuddling together then falling asleep. Marcheline took the other bed, but sleep didn't come quite as easily for her. She tossed and turned, one eye on the door. Her mind raced all night long, filled with thoughts of impending doom.

The nervousness surprised Marcheline, because in the years she had been living in Rosemary Run, she'd managed to maintain an even keel despite her precarious circumstances. But things were different now. And she knew they could get a lot worse before they got better. If they got better.

When daybreak arrived and it was time to get moving again, Marcheline felt relieved. Maybe she'd rest more when they arrived in Tucson to whatever safe haven Guillermo would provide them. She got out of bed and quickly showered and dressed for the day. She thought about everything happening in Rosemary Run and how her staff would look for her. She felt bad about Jim expecting her to Netflix and chill the night before, and about telling Leonard they would see each other soon when she knew they would not. Most of all, she worried she had let too much fall on Rande's shoulders. But she pushed all of that out of her mind and turned her thoughts towards moving forward. She had to. There wasn't another choice.

When Marcheline was ready to leave the hotel room, Sabine and Amelie were still sleeping soundly. The hairdryer hadn't even disturbed them. Marcheline left a note as she walked back across the parking lot to the truck stop to see if Carl was in yet. To her disappointment, Stu was still the attendant on duty.

"Stu," she said as she walked in the door and approached the counter. "It's a new day, my friend. And you're still here."

"Yeah," Stu said with a sigh. Marcheline got the idea he wasn't much of a conversationalist at any time of day. But she knew how to charm people and figured she had better get in good with Stu.

"Let me guess," he said. "You're here for Carl again."

"Smart man," Marcheline replied, grossly

exaggerating. She thought she detected a faint smile on Stu's face as he received the compliment, so her charms were working. "Is Carl in yet this morning?"

"Not yet," Stu said, sounding ever so slightly more enthusiastic. "But he'll be here any minute. And when he gets here, I can go home."

"I'll bet you're looking forward to that," Marcheline said, trying to strike up a conversation. She wanted Stu on her side. She had even thought about it in the middle of the night. Stu posed a risk, because he could report her to the authorities if he took a notion. It was *important* that she got him on her side.

"Yeah, you can say that again," Stu replied.

"Night shift is never fun," Marcheline continued. "I know that from experience, my friend."

"You worked night shift?" Stu asked. "You look too classy for that."

Marcheline laughed and tilted her head down. Her first instinct was to tilt her head back, but she was careful not to show her face to the security cameras. She was still wearing a ball cap. "That's right. I used to work at a gas station during college. And I worked the night shift plenty of times. Some strange people show up at gas stations in the middle of the night."

Stu leaned back on a stool, focusing his full attention on Marcheline for the first time. "Yeah, the crazies come out after dark," he said. "Some people are so high they can't even pay with correct change. Or else they move so slow it's like they've turned into sloths. Sometimes, I have to laugh out loud. They rarely notice when I do."

"I know what you mean," Marcheline added. "At the

gas station where I worked, some people would get so agitated that they were ready to fight each other in the parking lot. And I didn't want them fighting on the property. I would get in trouble if they did, even though I couldn't do much to stop them. It wasn't fair."

"Right!" Stu said, getting animated now. "I had to call the cops last week because some guys were fighting out by pump number two. I don't know what they were fighting about, but I don't think the dayshift attendant sees that kind of shit."

"I think you're right. Dayshift doesn't realize how lucky they are."

As Marcheline and Stu laughed together, a gray-haired Native American man wearing overalls and a straw hat walked in from the back. He was short and round, shaped like Humpty Dumpty. Marcheline wasn't sure what she had been expecting Carl to look like, but this wasn't it.

"Mr. Lowery," Stu said to the man, standing up straight. "Good morning, sir."

"Stu," the man replied as he tipped his hat. "And hello, Ma'am, good morning."

Marcheline squinted her eyes. She wasn't sure if he was calling her Ma'am on Rande's suggestion, or if it was a coincidence.

"Good morning," Marcheline said, extending her hand to shake Carl's.

His skin was pale and Marcheline suddenly became self-conscious about how dark hers was by comparison. She knew that some places in the country weren't as welcoming to brown-skinned folks as she was used to. She didn't know if she should be worried in these parts, but it concerned her that this was the first time she was thinking about it. She scolded herself and made a mental note to do more thorough preparation. She needed to be ready for every aspect of life on the run if she were to pull it off.

"This lady's looking for you," Stu said. "She was here last night, too."

"Is that right?" Carl asked, winking at Marcheline. "You look familiar, Ma'am."

There it was again. Ma'am. Marcheline thought it must be intentional.

"How do you know me?" she asked. "Do we have a mutual friend?"

"Mr. Pink, is it?" Carl asked. Pink was Rande's codename. It was somewhat unimaginative, but was chosen because his last name is Floyd. He had thought Pink Floyd was as good of an association as any, so he had decided to become Mr. Pink when a disguise to his identity was required.

"I do know a Mr. Pink," Marcheline confirmed. "An old cowboy from Wyoming. Does that sound like the same guy?"

"Indeed, it does," Carl confirmed. "Come on back with me we'll talk in my office."

Stu looked at Carl skeptically, eager to go home.

"Stuart," Carl began. "I need you to stay a few extra minutes and cover for me while I talk to this nice lady. I won't be long."

Stu's head dropped, but he reluctantly agreed. Marcheline was glad she had taken the time to chat with him. Hopefully, their rapport would offset his frustration at having to stick around longer than usual.

"Stu, you're a doll," Marcheline said warmly. She walked over and placed one hand on Stu's upper arm and looked him in the eye. "Truly, sir, you're very kind. Your help is much appreciated."

Stu smiled sheepishly, seeming content, so Marcheline followed Carl into the back. His office was small and dark, and it smelled like mildew. Marcheline was used to spending her time in much more swanky places that were clean and orderly. She told herself she'd have to get used to this and not make a big deal of it.

"Mr. Pink was in touch and he told me of your need," Carl said once the door was shut and it was just the two of them inside. "Short notice, so forgive me for not being able to get something nicer."

"Oh, don't worry about it at all," Marcheline said, and she meant it. "I'm just grateful you could get me something to drive. What is it?"

"It's an old red and white Ford Bronco. A gas guzzler," Carl explained. "Sorry about that. It seems to be in good working order for now. But unfortunately, I can't promise that it won't need some work done soon."

"That's perfectly fine, Carl," Marcheline said. "It just needs to get me to my next destination and I should be able to switch for something different there. Do you think it will carry me for a half day's drive?"

Carl nodded, and Marcheline suddenly wished she hadn't told him the distance she had left to go. Any scrap of information could lead to being found.

Carl could tell what she was thinking. "No need to

worry, Ma'am," Carl said. Marcheline was sure the nickname wasn't a coincidence now. "Mr. Pink and I go way back. I'd do anything for that old cowboy, and he'd do the same for me. He told me you were one of his. That's all I needed to hear."

"Thank you," Marcheline said simply.

"I don't know what you're involved in or what you're running from," Carl said. "But if I can help again, don't you hesitate to come back. Any friend of Mr. Pink's is a friend of mine."

Marcheline grinned as she thought about Rande and what a good friend he had been to her. She expected he would have been just as good of a friend to Carl. They were both lucky to know him.

"So, when can I get into the Bronco?" Marcheline asked. "Is it here now?"

"Almost," Carl said. It's being brought in from the Native American Reservation east of here. Shouldn't take more than a couple hours, max."

Marcheline squirmed when she heard this. She was getting antsy. She needed to get them moving.

"It was the best I could do, Ma'am," Carl added. "I'm sorry if it's not fast enough. Really, I am."

"It's okay."

"Are we making a trade? Mr. Pink mentioned that I would need to relieve you of your current vehicle."

"That's right," Marcheline said. "It's a Land Rover. Fully loaded. I hope you can make use of it. But it can't be traced back to me or even the location where I dropped it off. Can you make sure it gets shuffled to a different part of the country?"

"Can do," Carl replied. "The associate of mine who is bringing the truck will use his network to send it east. It will most likely end up at a reservation in Cherokee, North Carolina. It'll either be sold from there or used by someone in our network."

"Are you Native American?" Marcheline asked, curious.

"Yes, Ma'am," Carl replied. "Half blood, anyway. Hualapai. I have friends and family still living on the reservation. We take care of each other."

"That's really nice," Marcheline said. "I haven't seen my parents in over twenty-five years. The only family I have is my daughter. She's married now and I have a grandbaby."

Again, Marcheline felt bad having revealed so much information. And again, Carl could tell.

"Ma'am," Carl said as he leaned forward on his desk, placing his short arms in front of him. "You have my word. You can trust me. If anything harms you, it won't be of my doing. You're safe here. I won't repeat anything you tell me. You can... Relax."

Marcheline leaned back in her seat, eager to relax as Carl suggested. "I hear you," she said. "I'm just a little jumpy. That's all. I appreciate everything you're doing for me."

"It's my pleasure," Carl replied sincerely.

"Well, I guess I'll go back to my hotel room and wait. When the Bronco gets here, how will I know?"

"I'll have it parked beside your Land Rover. Keys will be under the mat. You shift your stuff on over, then leave your keys for me. We will have the truck gassed up and ready. You can drive away just as soon as you get in."

"Carl, you're a gem!" Marcheline exclaimed. Then she stood up, patted Carl on the shoulder, and headed back to her hotel room.

16

R yan had driven all night, downing energy drinks to stay awake. He had been so focused on getting to Sabine and Amelie before they left Kingman that he hadn't noticed Bill tailing him. Maybe it was because Bill had years of experience as a private investigator, following people without letting them know. Or maybe Ryan had been too naive to think he could be followed. Whatever the reason, Bill's track south to Kingman had been a success.

When Ryan pulled in the hotel parking lot, Marcheline's Land Rover was still parked outside. Ryan choked back tears when he saw it, knowing he'd found his wife and baby. He had been terrified he wouldn't make it in time.

Careful not to be detected, Bill hung back, then pulled in on the other side of the truck stop, not far behind.

Marcheline startled when there was a knock at the door. "Must be housekeeping," she mumbled. Amelie was awake now, but Sabine was still asleep. With the baby on her hip, Marcheline stepped up to the door to look out the peephole. She trusted Carl and his reassurances about how she was safe, so she wasn't worried. At least, she wasn't *too* worried. But she was cautious. Who could be knocking?

The color drained from Marcheline's face when she recognized the person standing on the other side.

17

"Ryan! Get in here," Marcheline said as she opened the door and pulled her son-in-law inside, looking both ways to see if anyone was watching.

Ryan grabbed Amelie from Marcheline's arms, then rushed to his wife and climbed into bed with her, cradling the two of them and holding them close.

"Marcheline, you had better have a damn good reason for taking my girls like this."

"Yes, I know and I do," Marcheline replied. "But first, we need to be sure you haven't been followed. Did you tell anyone you were coming here?"

"No," Ryan said. "Which was hard, because you know how close I am to my parents and my siblings. I had to resist the urge to pick up the phone. They will wonder what happened to us."

"Did Rande tell you what was going on?"

"Yes, he told me, generally. He didn't go into much detail."

"Did Rande tell you where to find us? Because I explicitly told him not…"

"It was me," Sabine said groggily, waking up. She hugged her husband tightly around the neck and kissed him on the lips. "I'm sorry, Mom," she said.

"Sabine!" Marcheline said, stepping close to the window and peering out. She wasn't sure what she was looking for, but figured she'd know it when she saw it. Hopefully.

"Marcheline," Ryan began again. "Are you sure you're not getting a little carried away here? This seems overkill. I don't mean to be disrespectful, but is everything okay with you?"

"It's more complicated than that," Sabine answered. Marcheline was glad to hear her daughter come to her defense, even though she didn't know the whole story yet.

"I hope so," Ryan replied. "I'd damn sure like to hear about it." He kissed Amelie on the forehead as she cooed, the three of them the picture of a happy young family.

"We tried to get to you before we left town yesterday," Sabine explained. "I called you a bunch of times."

"I was in a meeting with a big commercial client," Ryan said. "I'm so sorry I missed you. I had no idea…"

"It's okay," Sabine said, stroking Amelie's soft hair as she talked. "We will figure this out."

Ryan and Sabine watched Marcheline as she continued to peer out the window.

"Mom, what are you looking for?"

"I have to stand guard," Marcheline he said. "To make sure Ryan wasn't followed. And… I'm waiting on a truck. We will switch vehicles before we head further south."

Ryan and Sabine looked at each other skeptically.

"Where are we going?" Sabine asked. "I'm somewhat familiar with this area since I went to college at UNLV. There isn't much south of us. Phoenix, maybe? That's southeast."

"Good question," Ryan added.

Marcheline closed the shades and sat down on the side of her bed. "I'll tell you. But first, Ryan, I need to know where you stand. Sabine and Amelie can't go back to Rosemary Run. At least not right now. And now that you've disappeared, it's not wise for you to go back either. Are you willing to journey with us?"

Ryan looked thoughtful. "I'll do anything for my family. For Sabine and Amelie, and also for you, Marcheline, if you're really in trouble. But I want to know what's going on."

"And I'll tell you, in good time. Today, even!" Marcheline explained. "First, we need to get the truck and we need to leave both of our vehicles here. Rande connected me with a friend of his who is helping us make the exchange without being detected. The truck should be delivered shortly. When it gets here, we have to get in and go."

"How long will we be away?" Ryan asked. "Am I going to lose my job over this?"

Marcheline took a breath. "Ryan, my darling, you're not understanding the gravity of what's happening here. When we go, it will be with new identities. It's too dangerous otherwise. When we go, we're leaving our old lives behind."

"That's crazy," Ryan said, too fast to stop himself. "And it seems completely unnecessary."

"It is necessary," Marcheline said emphatically. "I promise you it is."

Ryan was quiet and seemed like he was holding something back.

"Say what you have to say," Marcheline assured. "I don't blame you for being mad. Or skeptical."

"I wouldn't say I'm mad," Ryan clarified. "I was mad when I first heard, but I've been driving all night and have had time to think more. Also, hearing you tell me that there's something more going on and having Sabine confirm it… I guess the mad is wearing off. But respectfully, Marcheline, I'm not sure you grasp the significance of taking my wife and child. You haven't been married. Have you? Because I don't think you get what that bond is and what it means."

This brought a tear to Marcheline's eye. Ryan was right, but he was wrong at the same time.

"I come from a loving home with two parents who have been married for most of their lives," Marcheline explained.

"Wait. You have parents?" Ryan asked. "Why haven't we met them? Amelie should know her great-grandparents."

"I didn't know either," Sabine inserted. "I should know my grandparents."

"Yes, I have parents," Marcheline said. "And I promise I'll fill you in as we drive."

Ryan sighed again. "I feel like we're talking in circles here," he said. He was a practical guy. He liked to get right down to business. It was part of what Sabine loved about him. He took action when others hesitated. He was a doer. "Marcheline, can you give me a straight answer, please? Where are we going when we leave here today?"

Marcheline leaned forward on her bed, matching Ryan's intensity. "I'll tell you as soon as you give me a straight answer. *Are you with us?* Are you ready to walk away from life as you know it and start a new life and a new identity, with us?"

Ryan leaned back and put one hand on top of his head, exasperated. "Marcheline, do you hear yourself? You sound insane. I mean it. This is insane."

Without skipping a beat, Marcheline realized it was time to be blunt. "I accused him of rape. He didn't do it. But now he's serving time in prison. If he finds out I have a daughter, he might think she's his and people will come after us."

"Holy shit!" Ryan replied.

Sabine sat up in the bed, eager to know more. "Is it Chester?" she asked. "So you're saying Chester is my father?"

"That's not what I'm saying," Marcheline replied. "But people will come after us. They'll come after you, Sabine! And the baby."

"People meaning Chester? And what's so bad if he does?" Ryan asked. "We can deal with that. There's no reason to run. There's definitely no reason to change our identities over it. Families deal with questions of paternity all the time. No big deal."

"There's more to it," Marcheline continued. "I was forced to say it was him. I was boxed in and had no choice. You've got to remember, Ryan, I was nineteen years old. I got into a bad way and a lot of things happened to me I've never spoken of. This is just one part of that puzzle."

Marcheline heard an engine outside, so she stepped to the window and peeked out.

"Our truck is here. We have to go."

"Is there really such a hurry?" Ryan said. "We're finally getting somewhere. Let's stay and talk a little more, and we will sort this out."

Marcheline looked at Ryan and mustered all the determination she had. "I've said enough. I'm leaving, and my daughter and my granddaughter go with me. I will keep them safe and will protect them with my life. I promise you that. If you want to come with us, then get in the car. But this is the last chance, Ryan. Once we go, we're gone."

Ryan looked at Sabine in disbelief. "Are you hearing this?" he asked her. "You're my wife, Sabine. Amelie is my child."

"Then get in the truck," Sabine said. Then she quickly washed herself and the baby, gathered her belongings, and followed Marcheline out the door.

18

B ill had managed to remain undetected, and he was pleased with himself. But he was getting tired. He quickly urinated in a grassy area while keeping his eyes on the hotel room and on Ryan's vehicle.

Bill was a planner. He was always prepared, and he kept granola bars and peanuts in every car he drove in case of a scenario exactly like this one. Luckily, he had picked some snacks up at the airport to stock his rental car with. He didn't have time to go into the truck stop now, because he would risk losing Ryan and family if he did.

He watched as Marcheline, Sabine, and Ryan loaded their things into the red and white Bronco and abandoned their other vehicles. When they pulled out of the motel and onto the interstate, he followed closely behind. Like Ryan, he, too, had survived the night by downing energy drinks. He popped another one open, telling himself it would all be worth it once he solved this mystery and, hopefully, restored his client's good name.

19

The day was growing bright and warm as Marcheline drove the Bronco southeast, deeper into Arizona. In some places, the topography looked similar to their home in California. In others, it was different enough to feel completely foreign. Much of the landscape they passed was desert. It was barren, but with a beauty all its own.

Marcheline thought the desert had a spiritual quality to it. For some reason she couldn't identify, it felt like she was on a quest to find herself. Even though it seemed counterintuitive given the reality of her circumstances, she began to think that perhaps the desert would somehow bring her peace.

Sabine rode in the passenger seat and Ryan rode in the backseat next to Amelie. They planned to trade back-and-forth when Sabine needed to breast-feed the baby. Ryan remained mostly quiet, and his silence caused Marcheline concern. She knew he was a smart guy and figured he was formulating a plan. It wouldn't have been like Ryan to go along with things blindly. He was the type who needed to see and know for himself before he could get on board.

They stopped for a late breakfast in the outskirts of Phoenix. It was fast food again, meat and biscuits this time. They went in and out quickly, careful not to spend too much time at any one place. They did their bathrooming, got their food, and got back on the road. Marcheline was eager to get to Tucson so they could get situated somewhere and get the baby out of the truck. It had been a lot of hours on the road, which was especially taxing for a baby. Amelie had impressed them all with how cooperative she'd been, but it wasn't fair to her. She needed room to stretch and crawl. She also needed a change of scenery.

As they passed through Phoenix and their surroundings became more and more desolate, Ryan broached the topic of Marcheline's past once more. They all knew they were nearing their destination and there were more questions that needed answers. Ryan was tactful in his approach, which Marcheline appreciated. She knew this was all her fault and she didn't take that lightly. Sabine tried to remain neutral, not taking one side over another.

"Mom?" Sabine began. She knew her husband was ready to talk. She wanted to be in on the conversation. "We're getting close to Tucson. Please tell us what's there. Why Tucson, of all places?"

"Yes, my darling," Marcheline replied. "I have more to explain. I know that. Thank you for being patient with me."

"We love you, Mom," Sabine said. "We really will get through this... Together."

Marcheline nodded. "Good. Tucson is where an old college friend of mine lives. His name is Guillermo Martinez. He promised me many years ago that if I ever needed to get away, he would provide me a safe place to regroup and start over."

"Does he know we're coming?" Ryan asked.

"No," Marcheline replied. "He doesn't. But he's the kind of friend... Well, we had the kind of arrangement... It's good anytime I show up."

"And does he know... Your story?" Sabine asked.

"He knows enough. The same as Rande. They don't know all the details, but they're privy to the most important ones. Guillermo knows the stakes. He has family across the border in Nogales, Mexico. If we can't stay in Tucson, he can get us across with a place to stay."

"My God," Ryan said. "Now we're talking about Mexico? That's even more intense." He was choosing his words carefully and trying to hold himself back. He didn't want to insult Marcheline.

"That might be what we need," Marcheline explained.

"Okay, so let me get this straight," Ryan continued. "We will show up at Guillermo's door. And you haven't seen him since college. But we will tell him we need safe passage to Mexico and new identities?"

"Pretty much, yes," Marcheline replied. "But hopefully, we can stay in Tucson or another U.S. city with our new identities. I don't intend to go to Mexico unless absolutely necessary."

"Mom," Sabine said. "Tell him your real name."

"Your real name?" Ryan asked. "What are you, in the witness protection program or something?"

Marcheline gripped the steering wheel again as she drove. The tension was rising. "Not exactly," she answered. "Or, I guess I should say, not officially."

"And what exactly does that mean?" Ryan asked. "Maybe you could just tell us instead of making us guess?"

"It means that I'm not officially in a witness protection program. But essentially, I created one for myself."

"And what made you do such a thing? Other than having falsely accused a man of rape. I can see how that would make you a few enemies."

"Stop it," Sabine said as she reached into the backseat and shoved her husband, her hand landing on his knee. "Easy."

"And like I told you," Marcheline said. "There's more to that story. I don't mean to sound melodramatic, but it's very difficult for me to talk about. So difficult, in fact, that I've never told another soul that part."

Sabine looked at her mom. "Do you want to pull over?" she asked. "Maybe you shouldn't be driving when you tell it."

Marcheline looked back at her daughter. Sabine was good to her mom. "That's very kind of you, and it's a great idea. There is a wide edge on the side of the road leading to open desert. I can pull over there."

At the next opportunity, Marcheline slowed the truck down and pulled off to the side. She left the engine running, but turned around in her seat to face both Ryan and Sabine. The heat from the sun felt warm coming through the windows, but not too warm to be uncomfortable.

"Go ahead, Mom," Sabine said. "You can tell us anything."

"Yeah, you can," Ryan said, although somewhat reluctantly.

Marcheline could tell Ryan was still strategizing. She thought he had probably gotten into the Bronco because he intended to solve this problem for her. He didn't seem to realize it was a problem that couldn't be solved.

Taking it slow, Marcheline filled Ryan in on what she had told Sabine the day before. She explained how she had come over from France with her parents when she was a toddler, and how her mom and dad were gone much of the time working hard at their bakery. She told him about getting involved with Chester and how she had always felt like an oddball in her school and neighborhood, how she didn't quite fit in.

"I never would have guessed," Ryan said when his mother-in-law was done. "Sabine, you didn't know any of that, did you?"

"No!" Sabine replied. "I didn't know Mom had lived in Illinois or that she had living parents. It was always a big mystery she didn't want to talk about."

"So, I suppose you'll want to hear why I would accuse Chester of... Raping me... When he didn't do it."

"Well, yes," Ryan said. "It's a pretty bad thing to do to a man. And you think he's serving prison time for the rape?"

"That, I'm not sure about," Marcheline said. "I've tried to keep up on the Internet, but I can't just search from my own computers. I have to drive to another county and go into a library to use theirs. I try not to do it often. I've been careful to avoid anything that could be traced back to me."

"Yeah," Ryan agreed.

"And you have to realize," Marceline continued. "Back when all this happened, the Internet wasn't really a thing. There was some Internet, but it wasn't all over like it is now. It was twenty-six years ago. Most people didn't have computers or if they did, it was just a word processor. When my rape accusation would have been investigated, tried, and possibly convicted, the case might not have been searchable on the Internet. Chester was from a bad part of town and people in his neighborhood were convicted of crimes all the time. My accusation wouldn't have made the news. It wouldn't have even been considered newsworthy because it was such a common occurrence in that part of Chicago."

"That's terrible, Mom," Sabine said. "I'm sorry you were involved in a situation like that. In a *place* like that."

"Thank you, my darling. But Chester was a good guy. That's why I wrote the letter to him. When you were a baby, Sabine, and I was in college, I was overwhelmed with guilt for what I'd done. It was all I could do to keep myself from confessing and going back to Chicago to turn myself in and take my punishment. But you were a baby and staying away... Staying hidden... Was the only way I could protect you."

"What about your parents?" Ryan asked. "Could they have helped with Sabine? I don't mean to sound like I'm complaining, because if they had, she and I probably wouldn't have met. So in a way, I'm grateful for that twist of fate and for your decision way back then."

Sabine gave her husband a knowing smile.

"And that leads me to the part that is so hard to say," Marcheline replied. "It makes me short of breath just thinking about it."

"It's okay," Sabine reassured, first placing her hand on her mother's shoulder, then leaning over for a hug. "You can tell us."

Marcheline stared out at the desert landscape around them. It almost felt like they were in a different world entirely. She didn't consider herself a religious person, but the spirituality of the desert was palpable and she wanted to tap into whatever strength she could as she spoke her truth. She closed her eyes and tilted her head back. Then she said a silent prayer to the powers that be for strength and clarity as she formed the words she had been holding in for more than half of her life.

"When I was a kid, we had a family friend who lived next-door. His name was Huey Moreau. He was so close to my parents that they deemed him an honorary uncle to me. So, I grew up knowing him as Uncle Huey."

"Okay," Sabine said, listening carefully.

"Uncle Huey," Marcheline continued. "He was French, too, having moved from Paris just a few years after we did. I guess my parents were eager to feel a sense of home in America. Perhaps they were too trusting for that reason alone. I don't know. But Uncle Huey... He..." Marcheline got choked up and had a hard time going on. "When I was just six years old, Huey began... Climbing into bed with me."

"Oh, Mom," Sabine said, tears forming in her eyes.

"My parents used to let him babysit me in the evenings. We'd all eat dinner together, but then my mom and dad would have to go back to the bakery to prep for the next morning. Huey owned a jewelry store, so there wasn't any night work involved. He was free in the evenings. My parents didn't know what was happening. They thought I was safe and that Uncle Huey was a good guy. But he was touching me and forcing me to touch him."

"That's terrible," Ryan said, his tone gentler than before.

"It's awful," Sabine echoed.

Marcheline glanced out the windows at the desert landscape again. It was anchoring her. "By the time I was thirteen," she continued. "He was giving me alcohol and marijuana. And having sex with me. He had a fishing cabin north of Evanston near the lake, and that's where the worst of the abuse took place. It was isolated up there. There was no one around to hear me cry. Or scream."

"My God…" Ryan mumbled. The car was silent as the weight settled over everyone. Amelie sensed the mood of the adults.

"I thought it was my fault," Marcheline said. "At age thirteen, you're not equipped to understand that you've been taken advantage of. Uncle Huey would have his way with me, then he would tell me I had asked for it and that I wanted it. He told me I was a slut and that my parents would disown me if they knew how I had seduced him."

Sabine bit her lip as she tried to hold back tears. "Did you ever tell your parents?"

"Never. I didn't want to disappoint them. But even more importantly, I didn't want them harmed."

"What do you mean?" Sabine asked.

"Uncle Huey's jewelry store was a front. He was affiliated with organized crime."

"The mob?" Sabine asked.

"Yes," Marcheline confirmed. "Huey told me that if I ever breathed a word about our... Encounters... He'd put a hit out on my parents and have them killed. And I believed he could really do it. I saw the businessmen who would come and go from his store. They were up to no good. They looked mean and scary. Worse than what mob characters look like on TV."

"Mom, that's so, so bad. It's heartbreaking."

"When I got involved with Chester, I did it because I thought he might protect me from Huey. I'm not sure I was thinking rationally back then. I was a kid. And I was an abused kid. But looking back, I know that was part of my motivation. Chester was a thug, basically. But as I said, he had a good heart. He was a good person who was wrapped up in thug culture because of where he lived. When we met and I started hanging out with him, he gave me an excuse to go somewhere that Huey wouldn't follow. It gave me a reprieve from Huey's abuse and unwanted advances, even if only for a few hours a day."

"Wow," Ryan said.

"When I became pregnant, I was dating Chester and having intimate relations with him, and also being raped by Huey. All unprotected, sadly. The honest truth of it, Sabine, is that I don't know which of the two men is your father. Neither one is the kind of father you deserve. And I'm so sorry for that. It's the biggest regret of my life. I've spent every day since doing my best to make it up to you. I hope you can see that."

Sabine sat stunned, unable to find words.

"Marcheline, we appreciate your honesty," Ryan said softly. "That must have been really hard for you."

Ryan put one hand on Marcheline shoulder and the other hand on his wife's.

"It was excruciating," Marcheline continued. "When I began to show towards the end of my first trimester, Huey noticed. He saw... When he would... Rape me. I had no way to hide my growing belly from him. I was completely vulnerable."

"No," Ryan said. "Marcheline, this keeps getting worse. I'm so sorry."

Marcheline's body heaved as tears made their way out. She tried to hold them in, but there was no stopping the flood. Ryan's kindness was more than she expected. His simple acknowledgment of her pain filled a void that had been waiting for many years.

"When you're ready, go ahead," he added. "We're here for you, Marcheline."

Marcheline took a moment to collect herself, then continued. "One night, when we were at Huey's fishing cabin and he noticed that I was pregnant, he... He beat me. Worse than ever before. He flew into a rage. He began by taking the belt out of his pants and lashing me with it as he chased me around the cabin."

"Oh God," Ryan mumbled.

"I ran from him," Marcheline continued. It was cold and I didn't have shoes on, but I ran outside. I ran towards the lake, dodging trees and cutting my feet on branches and rocks as I fumbled around in the darkness. I was in such pain, and I feared for my life. I ran down towards the lake, and in a flash, I suddenly considered drowning myself."

"Mom!" Sabine said, her first words in a while. "You were pregnant with me. You would have drowned me, too."

"My darling, Sabine," Marcheline he said. "That's exactly why I didn't do it. Somehow, I gathered the strength to get us out of there. I began to formulate a plan. It wouldn't be fast or easy. But I hoped it would work."

"Chester…" Sabine said.

"Yes. With the mob on Huey's side, I knew I'd never escape them. I needed a cover story to throw them off my trail and get Huey off the hook at the same time."

"Mom, I can't believe you had to deal with something like that when you were still a teenager."

"I had to grow up quickly."

"So, how did you do it?" Ryan asked.

"First, I made nice with Huey. That was the worst part of it all. I had to grovel and beg his forgiveness. It took time for him to believe me. I had to… Provide sexual favors. It was disgusting and horrible."

"You did what you had to do, Marcheline," Ryan said. "Don't feel badly about that. You're a survivor."

Marcheline continued. "Once Huey thought everything was back to normal, I explained to him that the baby was Chester's and couldn't possibly be his. I lied and said I'd been wearing a diaphragm when he and I had been intimate."

"And he believed you?" Sabine asked.

"He did. I had never so much as resisted him, so I guess he didn't think I had it in me to fight back."

Marcheline looked outside again. She needed more anchoring. The desert plants remained a comfort.

"Huey made it a point to remind me he could have anyone he wanted killed. He moved from threatening my parents' lives to threatening my own life and my baby's. I told him I had come up with a way to proceed so it would never come back on him. He pushed me to explain. I told him I would make it look like Chester had raped me and then I'd disappear. I promised I'd never return to Illinois and never ask him for anything. Chester would take the fall if someone had to. Satisfied, Huey let me go. When I got home, I packed my bags. The next morning, I said goodbye to my parents before I left for school. Little did they know, it was the last time I would see them."

"Oh, Mom," Sabine said sympathetically. "What were you? A senior in high school?"

"That's right. I was technically an adult, but nowhere near ready to leave my parents and be on my own. Except that I had no choice. When school was finished that day, I left with Chester. He picked me up in his Cadillac. I told him I was pregnant and that he and I needed to start a life together so we could take care of the baby properly."

"What did he say?" Sabine asked, animated now, apparently getting over the shock about her uncertain paternity.

"He agreed," Marcheline explained. "We went to my

house to get my car and a few items of clothing, then I moved into his building where he lived with an aunt. For two weeks, I lived there with them. I had to make sure that any physical evidence from Huey's rape was cleared from my system."

"Oh, wow," Ryan mumbled. "Poor Chester. Poor you. Horrible any way you look at it."

"I know," Marcheline said. "Finally, it was time to seal the deal. I hate that I did it, but I was trapped. I truly felt like I had no other option. I hope you know that. Both of you. I hope you can forgive me."

"Mom, it sounds like Chester is the one who needs to forgive you."

"You're right. I know."

"So, how did it… Go?" Ryan asked.

"I did what I had to do," Marcheline continued. "I initiated sex with Chester, and then I made it rough. So rough, it caused bruising and eventually bleeding. I'll never forget his face as he looked at me in disbelief. He had never been rough with me. He couldn't fathom why I was doing it to him. Later that night, I took some of his drug money. Then I drove to the emergency room. I went inside and I told them that my boyfriend had raped me. They took my statement and did a rape kit. I'll never forget the tears streaming down my cheeks as I went through those motions. It was one of the worst nights of my life, second only to the last night at Huey's fishing cabin."

"And I guess it was your word against his, right?" Ryan asked. "I mean, do you know what happened?"

"I don't," Marcheline replied. "When the medical

professionals were done and they let me leave the hospital, I took the cash and the few bags of belongings I had, then I got in my beaten up old car and started driving west. I never looked back. I couldn't."

Marcheline sat silently for a while, wiping tears from her eyes. Ryan, Sabine, and Amelie didn't make a sound, as if they were giving Marcheline space to recover from her confession. When she was ready, Marcheline suggested that they drive on, saying she was all talked out for a while. Ryan offered to take over driving duties and promised to continue on to Tucson without deviating from the path. Marcheline agreed and climbed into the passenger seat while Sabine moved to the back.

As Ryan put the truck in gear, then gradually increased his speed to get back up on the road, he noticed a small red sedan pulled over on the side, not far in front of them.

"Hey, that car looks familiar," he said. "There was one just like it traveling behind me last night."

Panic filled Marcheline's eyes in an instant. "Are you sure? I thought you said you weren't followed."

"Yeah, pretty sure," Ryan replied. "It was dark and desolate. There wasn't much to focus my attention on. So, I noticed the car. But I didn't think I was actually being followed. Although seeing the same car now makes me wonder."

Sabine looked at her mother, her eyes also wide with fear. "Mom!"

20

"Quick," Marcheline said to Ryan. "Drive! We need to lose him."

"Let's not get carried away," Ryan replied. "It's just a car on the side of the road. We don't know if the guy is following us."

"Was it a guy?" Marcheline asked.

"Yeah, definitely a guy," Ryan replied. "Short haircut. Looks like military or police. Probably former military or police."

"You saw his face?"

"At a gas station last night, yeah," Ryan answered. "If it's the same guy… It looks like it from the glance I just got."

Ryan accelerated to get up to Interstate speed, but wasn't driving as fast as Marcheline wanted him to.

"Ryan! You've got to go. Drive faster."

Marcheline was coming undone. Ryan and Sabine had never seen her like this.

"Mom, I agree with Ryan. Take it easy," she implored. "We don't know anything yet."

"You two are telling me to take it easy, but you don't understand. You don't know what the mob does to people. It isn't pretty. They're very creative about eliminating their enemies. They torture people before they kill them, and they rarely miss their marks."

"Okay," Ryan replied, trying not to sound condescending. "But are you sure that isn't dramatized for TV?"

Marcheline took a breath and tried to center herself. She knew she was spiraling out of control, and that Sabine and Ryan thought she was losing it.

"It's not just on TV," Marcheline said calmly. "You may not realize it since we don't really have organized crime in Rosemary Run. But back in Chicago, it's a huge problem. Maybe it isn't as bad now. I don't know. But when I lived there, it was rampant. And Huey… He held tremendous power within the organization. He could have anyone he wanted killed. I mean it. You've got to believe me."

"Okay," Ryan said. "We hear you."

"But do you *believe* me?" Marcheline asked. "You've to believe me."

Ryan and Sabine looked at each other.

"Tell us this," Ryan began. "Let's say the guy in the red car is following us and he is somehow connected to Huey and the mob. What do you think he will do to us? He's just one guy in a little car."

Marcheline leaned her head back on the seat, exasperated. She wiped her brow, which was beginning to perspire thanks to her nervousness. "It's not just one guy in a little car," she said. "It's about who he knows and who he tells. It's about them finding us. If that one guy knows it's us and knows where we are, he'll send for others. They'll come in the night. They blow people up in their cars. I'm telling you. This is so incredibly serious."

"So what do you think we should do?" Sabine asked. "You mentioned a private detective calling you at work yesterday, right?"

"Yes, that's right," Marcheline replied. "But it's not him or the authorities I'm worried about. If it were just the authorities, I would turn myself in. No questions asked. I would tell them what happened about the rape and clear Chester's name. Then I'd do my time or whatever punishment I needed to. I'm not afraid of punishment from the law. I'm afraid of punishment from the mob."

"You're afraid of Huey," Sabine confirmed.

Marcheline began to cry. She wasn't much of a crier. In fact, she rarely cried in her everyday life. She thought crying was a show of weakness, and she didn't like to do it.

"Mom, it's okay," Sabine reassured again. "We know this is emotional for you. We're driving to Tucson, just like you want. It's all going to be okay."

"Just drive, Ryan, please. Drive as fast as you can," Marcheline begged. Her hands were quivering. "Is the red car behind us? Do either of you see it?"

"No, not really," Ryan replied. "There's a car behind us in the distance, but with the glare from the sun, I can't make out any details."

They entered a stretch of road with a few other cars

on it. Marcheline knew from having spoken to Rande about the route that some of the way between Kingman and Tucson was a two-lane road rather than interstate. It made Marcheline nervous to be in such a desolate area. If the man was following them, he might try to trap them somewhere while he waited on others who would act as reinforcements. Marcheline knew she'd have to be extra vigilant. They couldn't leave the truck unattended, and they'd have to be very careful not to drive into any place they didn't have a clear exit. They'd have to sleep in shifts so that someone could keep watch at all times. Marcheline wondered how she would impress upon Ryan and Sabine the urgency of the situation and the need to remain on high alert. They just weren't getting it.

"We need to throw him off course," Marcheline said.

"What?" Ryan asked.

"Wait!" Marcheline exclaimed. "How is he tracking us?" She furrowed her brow as she thought. "Ryan! Your phone. You still have your phone, don't you? Give it to me, right now."

"No, Marcheline," Ryan replied. He was getting irritated. "We need a phone for safety. No one from the Chicago mob is tracking my phone."

"I said, right now!" Marcheline yelled. She leaned over from her spot in the passenger seat and got in Ryan's face as he drove. "Don't make me scare the baby, Ryan. Give it to me. The phone."

Ryan looked at his wife.

"It's just a phone," Sabine replied. "Mom has burners. We can use them if we need to make a call for reasons of safety."

Ryan glanced ahead at the road, then in the rearview mirror at the car in the distance. "Okay, you win," he said, reaching into his pants pocket and pulling out a smartphone. "Here you go, Marcheline. I hope you're happy. Because this is getting more and more ridiculous all the time."

Marcheline took the phone, crunched it with the heel of her boot, then rolled down her window and tossed it out.

"How could you be so stupid?" she asked her son-in-law. She had never talked to him in such a disrespectful way, but she was angry. And she thought he deserved it. "You're jeopardizing our safety. You're jeopardizing the safety of Sabine and Amelie. I don't even care about myself, Ryan. I promise you, I don't. I care about my daughter and my granddaughter. I thought you would do the same."

"Don't turn this around on me," Ryan said, raising his voice. "I am playing along with your little charade here. But it's getting out of hand. You need to stop and think about the effects of all this unnecessary drama. I'm just glad Amelie is a baby and won't remember this."

"Are you questioning my devotion to my daughter and granddaughter?" Marcheline asked. "Because that's what it sounds like."

"Come on, Marcheline. Cool it," Ryan said.

"Both of you, stop it!" Sabine said. "Fighting won't help anything. No matter what's happening, we need to stick together. We're on the same side here."

"Yeah, that's what I thought until yesterday," Ryan said under his breath. "Then she went off the rails."

"Stop it," Sabine said, more forcefully this time. "You heard what Mom's been through. You had tears in your eyes just a little while ago as you listened to her story. Don't turn on her now."

"I know," Ryan answered. "I did. And I genuinely feel for her. But I'm not sure she's thinking clearly. I'm no expert, but it seems like her past trauma is causing her to be paranoid. Sabine, do you really think somebody from the mob in Chicago is following us? Do you hear how absurd that sounds? And in a little car, no less. One guy. Wouldn't they send several guys in a bigger vehicle? I don't know. But this seems like an awful weak response for the mob."

Marcheline's whole body began to shake, she was so angry. Her words failed her. She didn't know what else she could say to explain to Ryan how dangerous the situation was. His inability to see the truth would put them at risk. She began to think they might need to get rid of him.

"I trust my mom," Sabine said. "She kept me safe and gave me a good life. It sounds like I would have been in danger if she'd stayed in Illinois. Who knows what would have happened to me? If she says we have to do this, then we do. Please, Ryan. Stick with us. Stick with me."

As the three of them contemplated their disagreement, the red sedan they'd seen pulled over was getting closer. The road was becoming twistier now, and it was filled with up-and-down hills. There were large cacti on either side, and it looked like a forest because the cacti were so tall and dense.

"Behind us," Marcheline said, gesturing backward.

"The car is following closer. It has to, so it doesn't lose us in this terrain."

Ryan glanced in the rearview mirror. "Alright, I'll give you that, Marcheline. The car and the guy definitely look like the same one I saw last night on my way to Kingman. He's following us. What do you want to do?"

21

Bill was growing weary. He hadn't slept, and he wasn't holding up well. He wasn't nearly as young as Ryan and couldn't handle a sleepless night with the same ease. The sun was blaring brightly in his eyes, adding to his wooziness. He needed a real meal, more than just snacks. And the curvy terrain was making him dizzy. He'd had to resort to urinating in an empty bottle he had in his car since the airport, but he'd need to defecate. He feared that he might soon have to find a container to vomit into if he couldn't get off the road and take care of himself. He didn't immediately see a large enough receptacle handy.

When Bill had gotten in the car last night to follow Ryan, he hadn't been prepared for all of this. He hadn't known where they were going. Not to mention, the truck ahead of him had three drivers. They could outlast him by a long stretch, and for all he knew, they were planning to drive across the entire country. He was getting desperate.

Bill hadn't told anyone where he was or what he was doing. He worked alone. The closest thing he had to a partner was a friend on the force in Chicago. Usually, he didn't get Gary Valcheck involved until a case was all wrapped up nicely, ready for an arrest. But this situation was different. Bill feared he was out of his depth, so he decided it was time to get his friend involved.

He pulled out the smartphone from his bag on the passenger seat and selected Gary's number. It took the call a minute to connect. Service was spotty. Finally, Gary's familiar voice greeted Bill on the other end of the line.

"Gary!" Bill said, relieved. "So good to hear your voice."

"Hey," Gary replied nonchalantly. "What's up?"

"I'm in a bit of a bind," Bill explained. "I want to tell somebody what's happening. Maybe you can do some investigating on your end to help me out?"

"That depends," Gary replied, giving his friend a hard time. "What are you into?"

Ryan was driving erratically in the truck ahead of Bill, speeding up and slowing down. He was probably trying to see if Bill would pass them and go on his way. The quick stops and starts were making Bill even more nauseous.

"I'm in Arizona," he said.

"What are you doing there?"

"I'm following a lead for a client of mine. It took me to Northern California first, and I thought that would be the end of it. But the son-in-law of the woman I'm tailing got into his SUV last night and tore out of town, so I followed. He drove all night long, then met up with his wife, baby, and mother-in-law here in Arizona. They got back on the road almost immediately."

"Are you by yourself?" Gary asked.

"Yeah, and I'm not sure how much longer I can keep this up. I don't know where they're going, but I need a hot meal, a bed, and to use some facilities."

"Are you sure the lead is worth all of this?" Gary asked. He knew Bill didn't like to give him any names until things had progressed further, so he didn't ask.

"I think so," Bill confirmed. "My client is serving time and his parents don't think he committed the crime. The woman I'm trailing wrote a letter apologizing for framing him something like twenty-six years ago. If that's true, it's a big deal."

"What was the crime?"

"You know how I do things. Nothing personal, but I'm not ready to disclose that yet."

"Fine. Why are they driving so far away? Are they running?"

"I can't be sure, but I called the woman at her office yesterday and spoke to her briefly on the phone. It seems odd that a long road trip would take place the same evening and into the next day. I mean, it seems fishy. Right?"

"You want to give me a name?"

"Not yet," Bill replied. "At least, I'm not sure yet. I haven't even talked to my client about it. His dad gave me the letter after it was received at his house a few days ago. This is all fresh. I want to learn more before talking to my client. I suspect this could be a case of an altered identity, and if so, I want to tread lightly. People don't go to all that trouble for nothing. I want to know what I'm dealing with before I make any decisions."

"Look, Bill," Gary said. "We've worked together a

long time and we've been friends for just as long. You can trust me with this. If you want to."

"I know."

"So what are you going to do? Do you want me to link up with local authorities? We can have a highway patrol car stop them."

Bill was silent as he considered his options. He knew they had a baby with them in the truck. He didn't want to scare the child.

"Give me a while longer," Bill announced. "Just be on standby, will you?"

"I can do that. I'll wait for word. We will mobilize a police response whenever you're ready. Sounds to me like that letter is enough reason to question them."

"Yeah," Bill agreed.

He was just about to hang up the phone when the truck in front of him came to a sudden stop, forcing him to slam on his brakes.

"Son of a bitch!" Bill shouted as the front of his rental car slammed into the back of the red and white Bronco, metal buckling under the force of the impact.

"You alright?" Gary asked.

"Yeah, dammit," Bill confirmed. "They slammed on their brakes and I rear-ended them. The son-in-law is getting out to talk to me. I've got to go."

Then he hung up the phone without waiting for Gary's response.

22

Ryan was guarded as he walked towards Bill's side of the car, but he wasn't afraid like Marcheline. She had told him she had a gun in her bag and had offered to let him carry it, but he refused. He didn't think he needed a gun for one guy in a little car. Besides, Ryan wasn't much of a gun person. Neither was Marcheline.

The force of the impact had apparently blown a gasket, because steam poured from underneath the hood of Bill's rental car. When Ryan reached the driver's side window, he tapped lightly. Bill was reluctant to roll the window down.

"Hey, buddy," Ryan began. "Following a little close there, weren't you?"

Bill stared at Ryan, still unsure.

"Do you hear me?" Ryan continued. "Why don't you roll your window down?"

Bill hung his head and put his chin against his chest. He wanted nothing more at that moment than to get out of the vehicle and stretch his legs, but he didn't want to compromise his investigation by interacting with Marcheline and her family. It wasn't the way private investigators did things. They certainly didn't rear-end the people they were tailing. He felt like a failure.

Ryan persisted, motioning for Bill to get out of the car. "Hey, buddy, I know you see me, even if you don't hear me."

Realizing he didn't have any other option, Bill finally unlocked the door and stepped outside. He put his hands up in the air, an indication that he didn't want any trouble and was unarmed.

"I'm really sorry about this," Bill said. "I was on my phone and wasn't paying attention. I'll pay for the damages."

"Do you think we're worried about the damages? To this old beater?" Ryan said with a laugh. "Looks like it did far more damage to your car. I'm more interested in why you've been following me. Best I can tell, you've been tailing me ever since last night… In California. And that's not a short drive. So, what's up?"

Bill hadn't realized that Ryan had identified him last night. He was at a loss as to how he should handle the situation. He had never found himself in this type of tangled mess before. He hesitated. Ryan was nearly a foot taller than Bill, and he was well built. Bill knew he would be no match for Ryan in a physical fight.

"Come on, man," Ryan persisted. "Just level with me. We're out here in the desert of Arizona, for Christ's sake. No one is around but us. And you just slammed into the back of my truck. There's no point in playing games. Just tell me what's happening. Why are you following us?"

"Alright, alright," Bill said, giving in. "I'm looking to speak to Marcheline Fay. She's your mother-in-law, right?"

"I don't know," Ryan said. "What do you want with my mother-in-law?"

"I spoke with her on the phone yesterday afternoon. I called her office. My name is Bill Henderson. I'm a private investigator based in Chicago."

"Wow," Ryan said.

"Here, let me get one of my cards," Bill said as he reached into his vehicle.

"Easy!" Ryan yelled. "Keep your hands where I can see them."

"Oh, right. Sorry," Bill added as he slid the card out from the console, then handed it to Ryan.

Ryan examined the card. Sure enough, it featured the name Bill Henderson, with a Chicago address and phone number.

"What do you want with her?"

"I was hired by the family of a man named Chester Loor. They think he may have been framed for a crime he didn't commit. He's serving prison time."

"What the hell does that have to do with my mother-in-law?" Ryan asked, even though Marcheline had already told him what it had to do with her. He was feeling protective of Marcheline, and he was surprised that this man had materialized in the Arizona desert. Bill had gone to a lot of trouble for a case that wasn't a big deal, which meant it probably was.

"My client's family received a letter from a Marcheline Fay."

"What kind of letter?"

"Well, I don't have a copy with me. But in it, she apologized for falsely accusing him. It was very heartfelt. Said she felt guilty about what she had done and didn't want him to suffer for it."

"So, you receive a letter and you're working a case, and it takes you from Chicago to California and then to Arizona? Do I have that right?"

"Yes, that's right," Bill said. "And at this point, I could really use something hot to eat. Maybe a good night's sleep and a bathroom?"

"Hey, that's on you for coming," Ryan said. "I'm not here to solve your bathroom problems."

Ryan looked hard at Bill, sizing him up. He was a middle-aged Caucasian man with greasy brown hair balding on top. He was in decent shape, but had a wiry build. He didn't look like he had the muscle to rough anyone up.

"Don't go anywhere," Ryan said as he walked towards the truck. "I'll be right back."

When he opened the door and got inside with his family, Marcheline and Sabine were eager to hear what had happened.

"Well?" Marcheline asked. She was doing her best to hold her temper and her anxiety down.

"He says he is Bill Henderson, the private investigator who called you at your office yesterday afternoon."

"Wow!" Sabine exclaimed. "Mom was right. We were being followed."

"I told you," Marcheline said. "Now will you pay attention and listen to me more closely?"

"He's probably not with the mob, but I have to admit,

I'm sorry I doubted you," Ryan said. "I didn't mean any offense, Marcheline. It just sounded so outlandish. But here we are in the middle of the desert, with a private investigator following us. You're onto *something*."

Ryan glanced in the side mirror to check on Bill. He was standing outside of his car leaning on the side. It was clear that the vehicle was no longer drivable.

"He's not going anywhere in that car," Ryan said. "Which means, we have to figure out what to do with him."

"You're exactly right," Marcheline agreed. "This is a critical juncture."

"Are you two thinking what I think you're thinking?" Sabine asked. "Are you going to… Hurt him in some way? Because that would be next level."

"I don't know," Marcheline replied. "Ryan? Your thoughts?"

Ryan tapped a finger on the steering wheel. He was becoming weary as well, having missed a full night's sleep. His thoughts were sluggish. "Okay, let's discuss our options."

"Good," Marcheline said. "Bill doesn't seem like such a threat on his own, but I'm concerned about who he has reported our whereabouts to."

"I agree he's not a threat on his own," Ryan said. "I could certainly take him, no problem. He's not a strong man… Unless he has some secret karate skills we don't know about."

They laughed, but immediately felt a little bad to be laughing in such a tense situation. They put on their serious faces and continued to brainstorm.

"So, we could leave him here and let another motorist find him," Marcheline said. "But then we don't know who he might talk to."

"Or we take him with us," Ryan said.

"Ryan!" Sabine replied. "We have a baby here. Our daughter. Do you want to bring some strange man to travel with us and *our baby*? A strange man who is after Mom, no less?"

"I hear you," Ryan said. "I'm not real comfortable with that myself, but we have to consider it. We could tie the guy up and put him in the back. And that way, we could do with him whatever we want."

"Guillermo would know what to do with him," Marcheline added.

"Guillermo in Tucson?" Ryan asked.

"That's the one."

"I guess the drive time would give us time to think further about how to handle the situation," Ryan said.

"I can't believe you two are actually considering putting a strange man in the car with our baby!" Sabine said, exasperated. She was feeling like a protective mama bear, and for good reason.

Marcheline and Ryan looked at each other. They had already made up their minds, regardless of Sabine's protest.

"I'm sorry, my darling," Marcheline said to Sabine. "It's the best thing for right now. There are too many unknowns and we can't risk leaving him. I don't want to hurt him, but we need more time to think. Ryan, do we have anything to tie him with?"

"My belt," Ryan said. "But let me be clear,

Marcheline. If we do this, we're committing a crime. If Bill wants to turn us in and press charges at any point, we're in a good bit of trouble. It's kidnapping."

"I know," Marcheline confirmed. "But I fear what might happen to us if we don't take him."

"Wait, let's slow this down," Sabine added. "Kidnapping is a big deal. How about we just offer the man a ride without tying him up? Mom, you could drive, and Amelie and I could move up to the front seat. We could leave Ryan in the back with Bill to keep close tabs on him. Ryan won't let him threaten us."

"Do you think he'd cooperate?" Marcheline asked. "Obviously, if he would, that would be the easiest way. If he thinks we're doing him a favor, then we aren't in any trouble. No crime committed."

"Sure. Why not?" Ryan asked. "You change seats and I'll go talk to him. But that begs the question. Do we still go to Tucson, or should we deviate and change locations?"

Marcheline lowered her brows as she thought. "That's difficult, too," she said. "We need to get to Guillermo as soon as possible. And he's in Tucson. But the more Bill knows, the more of a liability he is, and the more likely we'll need to silence him."

"Right," Ryan replied. "Do you have any other contacts in this part of the country? Does Rande?"

Marcheline he shook her head. "Not that I know of. When I thought about this day in my mind, I didn't anticipate a scenario like we're facing. It has me baffled, I admit."

"Can't we just drop him off at the next stop?" Sabine asked.

"That goes back to the problem of what he knows and who he might tell," Marcheline reiterated. She slammed both hands down on the dashboard. "Enough," she said forcefully. "I'll use one of the burner phones to call my friend Guillermo. We're less than an hour from Tucson and I might as well give him a heads up that we're coming. I'll ask him what he thinks we should do about Bill."

23

It had been even easier to reach Guillermo than Marcheline expected. She called the University, then asked to be transferred to his desk. Luckily, he was there, holding office hours so students could drop in. When he heard it was Marcheline on the phone, he ushered a young teacher's assistant out of his office and closed the door to give his old friend his full attention.

"Marcheline Fay!" he said cheerfully. "What do you know? I haven't heard from you in ages. How have you been, old gal?"

"Guillermo," Marcheline replied. "It's wonderful to hear your voice, my darling. It's been a while."

"Are you still in California?"

"Sort of, yes," Marcheline replied. "I own... Owned... A winery there. But things have taken a turn and I need your help. Does your offer still stand?"

She glanced out the rearview mirror as she talked, making sure Bill was still in place. He was there, leaning on the side of his car, apparently not planning to cause trouble.

"Absolutely," Guillermo confirmed. "My offer is good for life. You know that."

"I'm glad, my friend," Marcheline replied. "Because I'm about an hour away and I'm going to need the works."

Guillermo was silent. Marcheline got nervous for a moment, and she thought maybe someone else was listening. She knew this wasn't a secure line. But she was quickly relieved as she heard her friend scribbling down notes.

"Number of travelers?"

"Three adults and a five-month-old baby," she said.

"Okay, then. International travel?"

"Hopefully not, but we're open to that if you think it provides the best... Experience."

"Ages and genders, please."

Marcheline continued to provide Guillermo the information he requested, including eye colors and hair colors. She knew he was asking these questions to make fake IDs. She hoped it was safe to be discussing this level of detail on his school phone system. She had no choice but to trust him.

"There's something else," she added. "We have an uninvited guest. A white male in his late fifties or early sixties. I'm calling to not only tell you we're coming, but to also ask for your advice on how to handle the uninvited guest."

"Bring him to Tucson," Guillermo said without

hesitating. "If he doesn't like that plan, he can take it up with me."

"Wonderful," she said. "Where should we meet?"

"My brother owns a body shop in the industrial section of town. Martinez Body and Trim. Can you find it?"

"Yes, I'm sure we can."

"Good. I'll see you there. Five PM."

Satisfied, Marcheline hung up the phone, then destroyed the burner with the heel of her boot, and threw it out the window.

"Get Bill," she said to Ryan. "Put him in the back. We're taking him to Tucson."

"Tied?"

"I'll leave that up to you."

24

Ryan held his head high as he got out of the truck and walked back towards Bill. He knew he had the physical advantage, and he wanted to be sure Bill understood the pecking order. Ryan put his hands on his hips as he approached, puffing his body up to appear as big as possible. Bill looked at him expectantly.

"Can I offer you a ride?" Ryan asked.

Bill seemed relieved but hesitant at the same time. "Where are you headed?"

"I'm afraid I won't be able to tell you that unless you accept my offer. Even then, you won't know our final destination until we reach it. I'm sure you understand."

"Yeah," Bill said as he shuffled his feet nervously on the sandy ground. "I do."

"Good."

"What's the catch? I mean… What do you want from me?" Bill asked.

"No catch," Ryan replied. "To be frank, I'm not sure what we want from you yet. There's a lot we don't understand here. But we didn't think it was right to leave you in the middle of the desert."

"That's quite nice," Bill replied. "Especially considering I was following you."

"Yeah, well, don't get too excited. I'll be watching you like a hawk. My wife and baby are in that truck. If you so much as think about trying anything, well, then I'll handle you any way I see fit," Ryan explained. His tone was threatening, but appropriate.

"Understood. My phone isn't getting a signal here. It was connected when I…"

"When you rear-ended us?"

"Yeah," Bill continued. "But I can't get anything since ending that call. And I haven't seen more than a handful of vehicles pass since we've been parked here on the side. Not a single one stopped to help. So, yeah, I guess hitching a ride with you is my best bet."

"Okay, but you have to leave your phone here," Ryan said. "My mother-in-law insists. You can get it back when you return for the car."

"But…"

"No buts. No phone or no ride."

Bill fiddled with the door handle nervously as he looked around at the desolate landscape. He didn't have a better option, and they both knew it.

"Okay," he agreed, finally. "Let me just get my wallet out of my bag and I'll leave everything else."

He did that, then the two of them walked back to the truck, Ryan's hand on one of Bill's arms, guiding him. Marcheline and Sabine had already rearranged seats and were both up front with Amelie. Ryan opened the door to the back seat, then pushed Bill gently inside. Then he walked around to climb in himself.

Marcheline put the truck in gear and began to drive without so much as making eye contact with Bill. It was a bizarre situation for her to be in. She didn't want to be too friendly.

Sabine followed her mom's lead and stayed facing straight ahead in the passenger seat.

"Thank you kindly for the ride," Bill began, his voice soft and timid. He leaned forward slightly and directed his thanks to Marcheline.

"You're welcome," Ryan replied.

"I wanted to thank… The ladies," Bill continued.

"How about you communicate with me for the time being?" Ryan suggested. "We'll keep this simple."

"Okay," Bill replied. "But I'm not a bad guy. I promise you. I don't want this to be awkward…"

"You'll have to forgive me," he said. "But I have a hard time thinking a guy who followed me overnight and into the Arizona desert is a good guy. Do you get where I'm coming from?"

Bill nodded.

The truck was silent as Amelie chewed on her teething ring in her car seat up front.

"How old is she?" Bill asked.

Ryan shot him a look.

"I only ask because I have a granddaughter not much older. She's ten months old. Looks like your little girl is… What? Six months? They're a lot of fun at that age. They are little bundles of energy. And so curious about everything around them."

"Yeah. Right."

Bill went silent again, but seemed to have a hard time keeping quiet. He wanted to talk.

"My daughter… She's taking time off work to stay home with the baby. It's been the most fun to have them both around. Since my work schedule is flexible, I get to hang out with them."

Marcheline finally spoke. "If you're trying to find things you and I have in common, don't."

"I didn't mean to offend, Ms. Fay. And I don't want to be a bother. Like I said when we talked on the phone yesterday, I really just wanted to ask you a few questions. This has gotten out of hand."

Marcheline glanced in the rearview mirror, making eye contact now. "You know what? Go right ahead."

"Really?" Bill asked.

"Why not?" Marcheline replied. "We have time to kill."

"I don't think… I'm not sure…"

"Anything you would say to me alone can be said in front of my daughter and son-in-law," Marcheline clarified. "I'd like to know what was worth you tracking me down like this. So, you have my attention. Go ahead."

Bill looked at Ryan for permission. Ryan nodded. "She's the one in charge," Ryan clarified. "You'd be wise to do what she says."

Bill was a bundle of nerves. The more Marcheline thought about him, the more she felt sorry for him. He didn't appear to be much of a threat. Although she knew that his connections might be.

"Okay," Bill mumbled. "This is unconventional. But

I'll go ahead. Ms. Fay, I wanted to ask you about the letter you sent to Chester Loor. His father, Norman, received it and forwarded it to me."

"I told you on the phone," Marcheline replied. "I didn't send a letter."

Sabine opened her eyes wide and gave her mom a sideways glance, trying not to let Bill see her expression.

"That's why I said on the phone it was you or someone posing as you," Bill explained. "I fully realize that possibility. And I don't mean to accuse you of anything, Ms. Fay."

"And I told *you*, I don't know what you're talking about."

"Okay," he said, trying to figure out his next move.

"Who knows you were following me?" Marcheline asked pointedly.

"No one," Bill said. He sounded sincere. "I work alone, Ms. Fay. When I'm finished with a case, I take my findings to the appropriate parties. Those may include the person who hired me, the person whose defense my findings may support, and sometimes the police or attorneys involved. But I'm very careful. I never want to falsely accuse anyone or stir up something before I know exactly what's going on and what the consequences will be. I take pride in being accurate and careful."

"So you're telling me you followed us this far without another soul knowing what you were doing?"

"That's right."

"Kind of dangerous, isn't it?" Marcheline asked.

"Right," Ryan added. "We could be murderers, for all you know."

Bill looked at him, snapping his head away quickly. He wasn't sure whether to take Ryan's comments seriously.

"I don't know," Bill replied. "It's just what I do. I like to work alone. I've been doing it for decades."

"Who were you talking to when you rear-ended us?" Ryan asked. "You said you were on the phone and not paying attention."

"Well, now, I can explain that," Bill said. "I have a friend on the force and I called to tell him where I was."

Marcheline set up straighter in her seat, upset by this revelation.

"But I didn't tell him your name, Ms. Fay. I promise."

"Why should I believe you?" Marcheline asked.

"Because I'm a good guy. Like I told you. I'm an honest guy. I swear," Bill pleaded, trying hard to convince them. "Do you know a man named Chester Loor?"

Marcheline paused. She'd known this question was coming. She'd thought long and hard about what her answer would be.

"Mom, don't," Sabine said, her first statement since Bill had gotten in the car.

Marcheline looked at her daughter curiously. It was hard to get a read on what Sabine was thinking. She seemed to be on Marcheline's side. But she was curious about her father and wanted to unravel the mystery that surrounded him. Marcheline wasn't sure how Sabine wanted her to proceed.

Marcheline eyed Bill in the rearview mirror. "You're the one that's new here," she said. "How about you tell us more about yourself?"

Sabine nodded, happy with this diversion. Ryan shrugged his shoulders.

"Like what?" Bill asked. "What would you like to know?"

"I'd like to know how you ended up a private investigator, since you claim you're such a good guy," Marcheline began. "I mean, I'm sure there aren't *all* bad guys in your profession. But I don't exactly think of them as good guys either. What's the story there?"

"I started out in the military," Bill said. "I was military police. As a young man, I was sent to the Middle East to police soldiers stationed on active duty there. I guess I showed a curiosity not everyone has, and I soon became involved in military investigations. It was usually simple stuff, like answering questions surrounding soldiers who had gone absent without leave or those who had been involved in skirmishes. I didn't realize it at the time, but those little investigations showed me just how much I love the thrill of solving a good mystery."

"Sounds like you're a real American hero," Ryan said sarcastically. "We have a regular G.I. Joe, right here in our truck."

Bill laughed. He still wasn't sure how to take Ryan and was scared of him. But Bill also thought Ryan was funny. He liked his wit and the way he was protective of the women in his life.

"I served six years in the military, and then I returned home to Chicago. I actually attended a police academy for a short time as a rookie cop. But I knew it would take a while to work my way into investigations and I was eager to go ahead and get out on my own. So, I took the leap and hung out my shingle. I haven't looked back since."

"Do you follow any lead that someone pays you to follow?" Marcheline asked. "Or do you use your own judgment about what is worthy of your time?"

"Oh, I use my own judgment," Bill replied. "I have to if I want to stay in business. You know how that goes, Ms. Fay. You're a successful businesswoman. I'm sure you know all too well that you have to listen to your own gut. It's what carries you through the tough decisions and the hard times."

Marcheline smiled. "We can agree on that much."

"I guess you're wondering why I am here then, having followed you this far."

"Yeah, haven't we already said so?" Ryan added.

"I'll admit," Bill continued. "It was my gut. Something told me there was more to the story and that I needed to take a leap. Chester and his father seem like good people. I know Chester got mixed up in a lot of bad stuff. A lot of gang-related nonsense he never would have found himself in the middle of if he had grown up in a different neighborhood. But when I sit with him and talk with him, I just get a sense he is inherently good. It feels like he needs somebody on his side so he isn't overlooked by a system trained to forget about him."

Marcheline raised her eyebrows and shook her head. Bill had a good read on Chester, she'd give him that. She would have described Chester almost exactly the same way had she been asked.

"And I have to say," Bill continued. "I get the same sense about you, Ms. Fay. I researched you on the

Internet, and people say such glowing things about you. From all accounts, you're well-loved in your adopted hometown of Rosemary Run. Your employees are happy to work for you. And I can tell by being in your presence now that you're kind and good."

"That's very nice of you," Marcheline said. "I appreciate it."

"You're welcome," Bill affirmed. "That's why none of this adds up for me. Hear me out… Leena Bisset is the woman who accused Chester of rape when she was just a teenager. Now, granted, that's not all Chester is in for."

"It's not?" Marcheline asked, urgency in her voice.

"No, it's not. He's doing time for drug possession. Marijuana. It's a shame, really. If Chester lived in a state where marijuana was legalized, such as Colorado, he wouldn't be serving time right now at all.

"Oh, dear," Marcheline said, glancing at Sabine and then at Ryan. "Tell me more."

"The rape accusation put him on their radar. Chester was sentenced to supervised probation after that, and it was during that same period he failed a random drug test. They searched his vehicle and subsequently found a stash of marijuana. Since he was already on probation, it was an automatic conviction."

"Are you telling me that this Leena girl who accused Chester of rape isn't the reason he's in prison right now?" Ryan asked.

"Not directly, no," Bill replied. "But it was that rape accusation that got him into the system and sent him down the wrong path. Who is to say it wouldn't have happened, anyway? But I want to learn more."

"Then what do you hope to find by following us?" Ryan asked. "This whole thing seems so over dramatized."

"Norman Loor, Chester's father, won a large sum in the state lottery last year."

"Interesting turn of events," Marcheline remarked.

"Yeah, for sure," Bill agreed. "With his winnings, he hired me. Chester had always said he hadn't raped Leena. Even though knowing the truth won't change his drug conviction, Norman wanted to get to the bottom of it and clear his son's name. Not for legal reasons as much as, for reasons of the family's honor and good name."

"Although maybe, a parole board would have more compassion if they knew the whole story," Marcheline added.

"That's exactly it, Ms. Fay. If I were to find out *for sure* that Chester didn't rape Leena Bisset, I'd certainly bring that to the parole board's attention. Norman has hired a new attorney who would assist with that task. She's a good lady, too. No one has any ill will here. We just want to uncover the truth."

The truck was quiet for a few moments as this new information sunk in.

"Ms. Fay?" Bill asked quietly. "It seems to me like you have a really nice life in Rosemary Run. I stopped by your winery and your beautiful home. I'd sure hate it if you left town because of my inquiry."

Marcheline kept looking straight ahead. She didn't make eye contact with Bill this time. After an uncomfortable silence, Ryan spoke for her.

"Let's talk hypotheticals here for a minute, Bill," he

began. "Because I think you might actually be a good guy."

"Okay, go ahead."

"What if you found your Leena Bisset, and she confirmed that Chester Loor never raped her?"

"That would be great," Bill replied.

"And what if?" Ryan continued. "What if there were extenuating circumstances as to why she accused him in the first place. What if she were in danger from someone else, unrelated to Chester?"

"I can fill in some of those blanks myself," Bill replied. "Like, what if there was uncertainty about the paternity of Leena's unborn child, for instance?"

Sabine sniffled and wiped tears from her eyes. She couldn't help it.

"Hypothetically," Ryan continued. "What if you're right?"

"Then I'd want to assure Leena that I don't mean her any harm," Bill said. "I'd like to hear what happened to her so it could be explained to Chester, Norman, and the parole board that holds Chester's fate in their hands. I would also like to offer my assistance to Leena herself. If she were in danger, then I'd want to do my part to help protect her. And I would venture a guess that Chester and Norman would support me in doing so."

Marcheline's mind spun in a dizzying whirl as she drove the rest of the way to Tucson. She hadn't expected to be met with kindness like this. She hadn't expected someone in Bill's position to be on her side. She berated herself for having thought about harming the man. And she began to think about what Ryan had said about her trauma causing inappropriate reactions. She wondered if she was overreacting. Maybe she was even losing it completely. If she had exaggerated the danger, might her assessment of other things have been off? And if so, was she walking away from her happy life in Rosemary Run too soon?

By the time they arrived in Tucson, Marcheline was having second thoughts about turning Bill over to Guillermo. She was also having second thoughts about adopting a new identity without first assessing the threat more carefully.

With time running short and a lot at stake, Marcheline decided she'd have a heart to heart talk with Bill before meeting Guillermo at his brother's body shop. She pulled into a burger joint where they could sit together outside at a picnic table under a covered awning. She knew it would do them all some good to get out into the fresh air, and they needed something to eat. Ryan went inside to place an order for the group, while Marcheline, Sabine, Amelie, and Bill got situated outside.

Bill looked better to Marcheline than he had at first. He'd been to the bathroom and had cleaned himself up a bit, so that surely helped. But Marcheline was beginning to see him in a different light, which probably helped her impression of his appearance. It had been easy to think of him as unattractive when she thought he was a bad guy. But now, she noticed the crinkle under his eyes when he smiled, and the way his cheeks got rosy when he talked about his daughter and granddaughter. He was becoming human to her. He was becoming real. He was a man who people loved and respected. She could see that clearly now.

"Bill," Marcheline began as she sat across the table from him. "Have you been to Tucson before?"

"Never," he replied. "I suppose it's always good to see new places. How about you? Have you been here?"

"No, never," she replied. "But I have an old friend who lives here. In a few hours, we're going to pay him a visit."

A look of concern flashed across Bill's face. Marcheline could tell he still wasn't sure what she was going to do with him. She wasn't sure either.

"Bill," she began again. "What you said in the truck has really touched me. I think I underestimated and misunderstood you." She flashed him a sincere smile. "The friend I'm meeting here has the connections and the capabilities to make you disappear. Now, I know that sounds scary, but I was prepared to do whatever I had to in order to protect my own daughter and granddaughter. At this point, I imagine you probably understand that."

"I do, Ms. Fay," he replied adamantly. "I absolutely do. But yes, it does sound scary. My wife... She passed away three years ago and I need to stick around for my daughter and granddaughter. I'm not even concerned about myself as much as I am them. They need me."

"Then I think we understand each other perfectly," Marcheline said.

"Sounds like we do."

Marcheline put one hand on her head as she leaned forward on the table and braced herself for what she was about to admit. Sabine sat down beside her mother, holding Amelie on one knee.

"Mom, I'm right here," Sabine said. "Go ahead. It's okay."

Ryan arrived with their food, and they ate burgers and French fries like hungry teenagers, giving Marcheline a temporary reprieve. When they were finished, Sabine looked at her mom and then gestured towards Bill. "Go ahead, Mom."

Marcheline looked at her daughter, then at Ryan.

"Hey," Ryan said. "I'm just along for this ride."

Marcheline nodded then laced her fingers in front of her.

"Can I trust you, Bill Henderson?" she asked. "I mean *really* trust you?"

"Yes, you can."

"Because if I can't, as I mentioned…"

"Wow, did you threaten him while I was getting our burgers?" Ryan asked.

"We understand each other, Ms. Fay," Bill said.

"Please, you may call me Marcheline."

"Okay, Marcheline," Bill said, using one hand to pat the top of hers briefly. "Tell me what it is you want to say."

"This is hard," she began. "Harder than I imagined."

"Take your time," Bill said. "I'm not going anywhere." He chuckled at his own remark, amusing himself.

"Okay," Marcheline said hesitantly. She took a deep, full breath and then began. "I am Leena Bisset."

"Yeah, I got that idea," Bill confirmed.

"You're right. I accused Chester Loor of raping me, but he didn't do it."

"Then tell me why, and we can sort this all out."

Marcheline explained in detail the same way she had to Sabine and Ryan that morning. She told Bill about Huey's abuse and the night at his fishing cabin when he found out she was pregnant. She went through the story in excruciating detail. It was painful for her, but it was also cathartic. By the time she was done, they were all in tears.

"Ms. Fay… Marcheline," Bill said, his voice full of compassion. "I'm so sorry that happened to you. You were just a kid. You didn't deserve any of that. It's horrible. Frankly, I think Huey Moreau should burn in hell for what he did."

"Thank you for saying that, Bill," she replied. "I think you are a good man."

He smiled. "Did you ever tell Chester what was happening with Huey?"

"Never," she said. "I never told anyone until I told my daughter and son-in-law this morning. You have to understand, Huey told me it was my fault. He told me I wanted it and was asking for it. When you grow up hearing that, you believe it. When Huey first began abusing me, I was far too young to make any sense out of such a complicated dynamic. Besides, he made it a point to threaten me regularly. I honestly thought Huey would kill my parents if I told anyone. And then I thought he would kill my daughter. And by extension, my granddaughter. I still fear him. That's why I am running away. Again."

Bill looked at Ryan, and the two of them seemed to be communicating without words. Marcheline got the idea they could see through her pain and were assessing the reality of her fears. She knew they had good intentions and didn't mean to minimize what she'd been through, but she could sense that her thoughts were clouded on the topic. Ryan was right. The trauma still had a hold on her. She was making decisions from a place of fear.

"Marcheline, dear," Bill continued. "About how many miles away from home are you right now?"

The question caught Marcheline off guard. New tears formed in her eyes. "From Rosemary Run, about nine hundred miles," she said.

"And from Evanston?"

Marcheline raised one hand and put it over her mouth. She was too choked up to speak.

"Were you close to your parents?" Bill continued.

Marcheline nodded hard.

"She said they were wonderful parents," Sabine added, speaking for her mom. "They didn't know about Huey."

Bill leaned forward, further across the table. "Would you let me help you?"

"How could you possibly do that?" Marcheline asked, her voice breaking.

"I could use my expertise to look into Huey. We can find out what he's doing and what his situation is now. There might be a way that we can get everything out into the open so you wouldn't have to run anymore."

Marcheline closed her eyes as she continued to cry. Not once in the twenty-six years since she had fled the state of Illinois had she thought everything might be okay. She could hardly imagine it now, but something about Bill made her trust him. A part of her thought maybe he could really help. Maybe everything could turn out well in the end.

"But, the mob?" Marcheline asked. "You live in Chicago, Bill. You know what it's like there. I don't think my daughter and son-in-law fully appreciate the seriousness of the threat."

"I hear you," Bill replied. "And I definitely appreciate the seriousness of that threat. But there are circumstances that might make it a non-issue."

"Like?"

"Not to be too forward here," Bill continued. "But the paternity of your daughter is a big unknown. If Chester is her father, then Huey doesn't have any reason to be concerned. His secret stays hidden. Unless you decide to go after him and try to make him pay for his crimes. But that's a separate issue."

"It makes me nervous," Marcheline said. "I think any indication that Leena Bisset is alive and well could prompt Huey to send his people after us. I just can't take that risk."

Bill sighed and looked at Ryan again. Then he put his hand on top of Marcheline's, letting it rest there this time. "You know, that happened a long time ago. Huey might not even be around anymore. For all we know, the man's dead. Or senile. How old was he, last you knew?"

"I'm not sure," Marcheline said. "He was older than my parents. They were in their forties, so he might have been in his fifties?"

Bill smiled. "Marcheline, honey, add twenty-six years to that and the man has to be at least eighty-five years old now. If mobsters live that long, it's unusual for them to remain actively involved. If Huey has any memory problems, for instance, the organization would have stopped paying close attention to his directives."

Marcheline nodded her understanding. She had never thought about it that way. In her mind, Huey was still the same, frozen in time. It was difficult to think of him at all, but it made her feel a little better to picture him as an eighty-five-year-old man. He wouldn't be able to physically dominate her anymore.

"And I don't mean to question your judgment," Bill continued. "Please, know that's not what I'm saying here. But you were young and afraid. Once a kid loses their power, it becomes easy for an adult to continue to manipulate them. Are you sure Huey was even in the mob to begin with? Could he have just told you that to better control you?"

Marcheline sobbed now, her whole body heaving and quivering. The thought of Huey's mob involvement being nothing more than a mind game had never crossed her mind, and she was embarrassed that it hadn't. It made so much sense as Bill said it matter-of-factly, but it had been the farthest thing from Marcheline's troubled mind. Maybe she imagined the shady-looking men going in and out of Huey's jewelry store. Maybe it all just seemed scary since he was abusing her. Maybe he had lied to her, saying exactly what was needed to keep her afraid.

Sabine handed Amelie to Ryan, then she wrapped her arms tightly around her mom. Sabine cried along with Marcheline as the reality of how badly she had been hurt sunk in. Bill kept his hand on Marcheline's. Ryan stood up with the baby and walked behind Marcheline, then placed one of his hands on her shoulders. They enveloped her, placing themselves around her and reaching out to provide comfort and a loving touch.

Marcheline had stayed walled off from people for as long as she could remember. Even the people closest to her hadn't known the whole truth. She had believed they wouldn't love and accept her if they'd known. For the first time, she was beginning to realize just how wrong she had been.

"We love you, Mom," Sabine said. "Maybe Bill was sent to help you. Have you thought of that?"

Marcheline looked at Bill. He shrugged his shoulders.

"You know I'm not religious," Sabine added. "But I'm a believer in fate and things that are beyond what we can understand. Something is clearly at work here. Bill had to literally slam into our vehicle in the Arizona desert to get to you, but he's here. I think you should let him help."

"Yeah, Marcheline," Ryan added. "We love you. You're loved by a lot of people. It's about time that you were able to heal from everything that's happened to you. You deserve that. And you deserve to live in peace without having to look over your shoulder, ready to leave town at a moment's notice."

"Yeah, Mom," Sabine continued. "And I deserve to know who my father is."

Marcheline sputtered and choked as Sabine said those words. "I'm sorry, Sabine. I really am. I never wanted to deprive you of a father. It was an impossible situation. It *is* an impossible situation."

"Mom, it's okay. I know I keep saying the word okay, but it is. If Chester is my father, then I'll get to know him. It sounds like he's a good guy who has had some tough breaks. I can handle that."

"Chester and Norman would be over the moon," Bill replied. "Chester doesn't have any other children."

Sabine smiled at the thought of it. Maybe Chester wasn't what she had pictured as an ideal dad, but she understood that's how life works sometimes. She was capable of looking at the bright side and finding the best in the situation.

"You said you told him you were pregnant and that the two of you should raise the baby together, right?" Sabine asked.

"At first, yes," Marcheline replied. "But then I told him

I'd lost the baby. I didn't want him trying to find me either. I know it was wrong to do."

"It's in the past now," Sabine said. "I understand why you did what you did."

"I'm glad, my darling."

"And, Mom, if it's Huey… If he's my father… Then that's okay, too. It's not my preference. But you've been such a good mom to me. You've been parent enough for the both of you. You stepped up in every way imaginable and have given me the best childhood I ever could have asked for. I don't blame you, Mom. I can handle this. We can get through it together."

26

"Give me a day," Bill said. "Let's find a place to stay and then let me get my hands on a phone and a laptop. I'll do some digging with the help of my friend Gary on the force in Chicago. I promise you can trust him, too."

"What about…?" Sabine began.

"If you'll allow it, I will take a swab of cells from the inside of your cheek and will express ship them to Gary. He can have the lab test your DNA against Chester's. If it's not a match, then we'll move on from there."

"Do it," Sabine instructed.

Bill could sense Marcheline's hesitation. "Marcheline, no one will trace anything back to you. I won't give them names unless and until you're ready. I promise."

"Alright," she said, all cried out. "I trust you."

When they all climbed back into the truck, Marcheline used another one of her burner phones to call Guillermo and tell him she wouldn't be at the body shop at five o'clock. She explained that his help, offered all those years

ago when they were college friends, might not be
necessary. He took the information in stride, sounding
confused, but relieved for his friend. He said that since
they were in Tucson, they might as well come to his house
for dinner. His wife Camila was from Mexico also and
Guillermo said she was a great cook. He insisted that his
wife loved to entertain guests and wouldn't mind the
imposition. Marcheline agreed, promising to arrive
around seven with wine in hand. Bottles manufactured by
Maison du Vin were sold at a local mom-and-pop grocery
store. She promised to pick one up and give her friend a
taste of the fruits of her labor.

With those plans in place, the group found a
comfortable hotel that was much nicer than the rundown
places they stayed when they had been avoiding attention.
The Old Pueblo Inn and Suites boasted views of the
iconic Sentinel Peak. The grounds were landscaped with
the most stunning desert plants Marcheline had ever seen.
The lush swimming pool area was like an oasis, filled with
flowers, singing birds, and stunning architecture. Ryan
noticed right away and complemented the developers on
the green design that blended so beautifully with the
natural landscape of the area. Hotel owners had spared
no expense on their facility or the amenities it provided.
The place was a true retreat, and it was exactly what
Marcheline needed. All the way down to the small batch
hand soap and bath care items placed in each suite, the
Inn was a joy.

They rented three rooms, one for Bill, one for
Marcheline, and one for Ryan, Sabine, and Amelie.
Marcheline generously offered to pay for all three, telling

the group it was the least she could do after having dragged them down there, nearly to the Mexican border.

Bill called for a rental car, then went out shopping for clean clothes, a new phone, and a laptop. He returned shortly thereafter, then cleaned himself up and got down to work in his suite. As promised, he had purchased a vial and swabs for Sabine's cheek. Once her cells were placed inside, he packaged the vial up for safe transit, then left it with the concierge with instructions to get it to Gary as soon as humanly possible. Bill still hadn't slept, a fact that wasn't lost on Marcheline. His dedication to helping her even while exhausting himself in the process meant a great deal.

Ryan napped while he waited until it was time to go to dinner, so Sabine took Amelie to the pool. It was much warmer than Rosemary Run this time of year and she enjoyed the chance to let the baby experience the water.

While Bill was working and everyone else was enjoying the downtime, Marcheline got a pen and paper from the desk in her suite, then began to write a new letter.

27

Dear Uncle Huey,

I never intended to speak to you again, not even in a letter. I did my best to strike you from my consciousness and to never think your name, let alone speak or write it. But you were always there in the background, creeping in.

You took my innocence as a young girl and every day since. Like a disease, you spread throughout my being, wrecking every fiber and dampening anything good. I couldn't shake loose from you, no matter how hard I tried.

To say I hate you is an understatement.

I don't know what you think of me. Maybe you think I was too young to remember your abuse, or that it wasn't that bad. But I remember every moment of it. I remember being a young girl, six years old and just beginning to feel independent in the simplest of ways. My parents loved and cared for me. They cherished me, their most precious little darling. I know the feeling, because I felt the same about my own daughter. But you, you broke their trust and mine when you began climbing in my bed and putting your filthy hands on my innocent young body.

What, you think I didn't remember?

I remember the first time. I had fallen asleep, only to be awakened to your hand underneath my shirt. It felt wrong and vile, but I was too young to understand why. Then, when you put your hand down my pants and touched me in my most sacred of places, I couldn't explain why I'd gone to the bathroom and thrown up afterwards. But my body knew.

As I got older and the touching continued, I remembered every time.

I remember the first time you pulled down your pants and made me touch you. I didn't realize that my chronic stomach aches and bedwetting in elementary school were a direct result.

I remember the first time you penetrated me. Sure, I didn't push you away or yell or hit. I didn't know I could. By then, you had threatened to have my parents killed if I told anyone. I loved them dearly and would never have put them at risk, so instead of speaking up, I cried silently as you heaved on top of me, your filthy breath and bad body stench assaulting my senses.

And then at the end of us, the last day I saw your disgusting face, I remember. It was at your fishing cabin, where you not only raped and violated me, but you beat me and you chased me, making me fear for my own life and that of my unborn child's. That's in addition to the fear for my parents' lives, *which never went far from the front of my consciousness. Did you know that on that night, when I ran down by the lake, I considered going in and forcing myself under the cold water until the pain stopped? If it hadn't been for the baby growing inside of me, I probably would have done exactly that. And all thanks to you, Huey. I never would have been in such a fragile state if you hadn't wormed your way in without my parents' knowledge and then manipulated and violated me in the worst possible ways.*

Do you realize that I've been incapable of having a healthy romantic relationship? That's all because of you. I've dated good men, but I don't let them get close to me. I've never married. I've never been called someone's wife. I've never felt the excitement of having an engagement ring slipped onto my finger. I've never seen the look on my dad's face as he walked me down the wedding aisle. And every time I make love, it feels a little sickening, a feeling I can't completely explain, but it's there. Because of you.

But I want you to know that even though you took so much from me, I wouldn't let you take it all. I ran away, and I started a good life for myself and my daughter. I knew I was smart and I used my intelligence. I went to college on student loans, and I struggled as a single mother. But I finished my business degree, Huey. You didn't stop me from that. Then, I settled in a friendly town with a new identity so you could never find me. And I did well in that town. I made friends. I opened a business that's now thriving providing wealth and financial security for me as well as jobs for many others.

You took a part of me. You took me from my parents, because I was afraid that you'd kill us if I didn't disappear. But Huey, I have a strength deep down inside that you could never completely take away. I haven't let you take the best of me. I told a bold lie that I'll apologize to Chester for. But I'll never feel bad about what that lie did for me and my baby. It got us away from you.

A self-help guru on an Oprah Winfrey Show inspired me a long time ago to write a letter. She suggested it go to those I've hurt, or those who hurt me. She said any unfinished business could be healed, even if the letter was never sent. At that time, I couldn't even think about you in the conscious part of my mind. At least, not on purpose. So I wrote a letter to Chester. Poor Chester. He didn't deserve what happened to him. I never should have told anyone that he raped me when he didn't. But the thing is, in some strange and wondrous way, that letter brought me to this moment. It brought me healing that I didn't know I needed. I've been content to keep you out of my mind as much as I could and to carry on with my new identity. But now, I realize the person I should have written a letter to a long time ago was you.

Let me make myself clear. You are the most wretched scum to walk this earth. Those who take advantage of children and sexually abuse them are the worst of the worst. But something is changing in me. No longer will I let you terrorize me and hide me from everything I deserve in life. I'm choosing to make decisions from a place of love instead of fear. I'm choosing to let good people help me, beginning with Bill Henderson.

It's over between us, Huey. I'm stepping into the light.

Never yours,
Leena Bisset

28

W hen Marcheline was finished with the letter, she folded it up and tucked it into her handbag. Feeling inspired by the desert landscape around her, she decided to go outside and sit by the pool. Sabine and Amelie had returned to their room by the time she got there, but she didn't mind. She wanted a few more minutes alone.

To Marcheline's surprise, the water called to her. She *had* to do more than sit nearby, even though she hadn't packed a swimsuit. She was wearing yoga pants and an old t-shirt, which she decided would do. No one else was around, so she figured no one would mind, anyway.

As she walked into the water, it felt cool and refreshing, but not too cold. It felt silky. It felt like it was beckoning her, to connect her with something bigger.

Once she reached the center of the pool, she stood with her feet shoulder width apart, staring out into the desert with the mountain in the distance. She closed her eyes and let the afternoon sun shine on her face as she allowed her mind go blank and her body to go still. She thought about the time she had almost ended her life in that Illinois lake and about how water could both give life and take it away.

As Marcheline gently descended into a meditative state, her pain that had been locked up tight inside her body seemed to unhinge. She swayed in the water, her gentle movements matching the energy she sensed swirling around her. She could feel the energy emanating from the desert plants and stones. It was a different energy than she was used to at home in California. And it was doing something *to* her. It was doing something *with* her.

Marcheline stayed like that, standing in the pool and swaying gently while the sun shone on her face and the energy swirled around her, for what felt like an instant and an eternity at the same time. When she finally opened her eyes, a certainty settled over her. She knew she had been changed.

29

By the time Marcheline, her family, and Bill gathered in the hotel lobby to head to Guillermo's house, the sun had set and the last lingering bits of light illuminated the sky in a beautiful pink. Bill offered to drive everyone in his rental car, since it was nicer and more comfortable than the old beaten up Bronco. He had sprung for a full size so he could make the offer.

Marcheline got in the passenger seat, while Sabine and Ryan got in the back along with Amelie and her car seat. They were dressed in several different types of clothing, due to the haphazard nature of the way they had packed. No one had been thinking about a dinner party when they'd thrown some clothes in bags the night before. Even so, Marcheline thought they cleaned up nicely. She was wearing a black t-shirt with a cable knit shawl over top, along with jeans and sandals. It would have to do. Ryan and Sabine looked a little nicer, Sabine wearing a skirt and Ryan with a collared shirt. Bill was dressed the nicest of them all since he'd had the benefit of knowing about the dinner party when he'd stopped at the store this afternoon. He wore linen pants, nice shoes, and a long-sleeve, button-down shirt.

No one said much on the ride over. There was a quiet contentment amongst them they didn't want to disturb. As promised, they stopped to pick up some Maison du Vin wine bottles, Sabine going into the store with Marcheline while Ryan and Bill stayed in the car with the baby. Once the wine was in hand, they continued on to Guillermo's house for the special evening.

Guillermo's home sat on top of a hill that overlooked the city. It had a stately appearance, much like Marcheline's estate. Lights illuminated the long walkway to the front door and a broad porch sat ready to greet guests. Marcheline found it magical as the car climbed the steep driveway and more and more lights unfolded in the distance. She was proud of her friend for having done so well for himself. They had both come a long way since the days of scrimping as poor college students.

Marcheline felt excited as she got out of the car with her crew and walked up to ring the bell. She wondered if Guillermo would still seem the same, just an older version of himself. A pleasant looking woman arrived at the door first, then opened it and introduced herself as Camila.

"Welcome!" she said in a sweet voice. She was all smiles, her long brown hair swaying as she moved. "I am Camila, wife of Guillermo." She had a Spanish accent that made her all the more charming.

"Hello, Camila!" Marcheline said, handing her the bottles of wine. "We brought these for you. They were made by my own winery in Northern California, Maison du Vin."

"Oh!" Camila replied. "Yes, good. I will love. Me Encanta!"

"Buena!" Marcheline said, using her rudimentary Spanish skills.

Guillermo appeared behind his wife in the doorway with a big smile on his face. He looked as handsome as ever, his strong features and silky black hair on display. He gently moved Camila to the side so he could get to his friend. "Marcheline, it's been too long," he said as he kissed her gently on the cheek.

Marcheline beamed, she was so happy to see her old friend. She wrapped her arms around his neck and hugged him tightly. She didn't want to let him go.

"Come now, introduce me to your family," Guillermo prompted.

"They are my pride and joy," she said. "My daughter, Sabine. My son-in-law, Ryan. And their baby girl, Amelie."

"And our friend, Bill Henderson," Sabine added.

"Yes," Marcheline agreed. "Our new friend."

"Is this the uninvited guest you mentioned?" Guillermo asked.

"It is," Marcheline confirmed. "But he's no longer uninvited, that's for sure."

They went inside, and Marcheline admired Guillermo and Camila's house. It was every bit as gorgeous on the inside as it was on the outside. Guillermo credited Camila for her good taste in decor. He said that before she came into his life, he was living in a small apartment with nothing on the walls but a drug-store calendar. Camila was a gracious host and seemed to enjoy having everyone at her home.

"Do you like?" Camila asked as she showed the group to the formal dinner table. It was placed in front of sliding glass doors that led to a large deck with the most amazing view. The table was set with colorful Mexican dinnerware. Each piece was detailed and intricate. Marcheline thought they were probably handmade.

"Yes!" Marcheline replied. The group agreed, nodding their heads and opening their eyes wide.

"Beautiful," Sabine added.

"Guillermo," Marcheline began. "I get the feeling we're about to have the best Mexican food we've ever eaten."

"I don't know," he said with a chuckle. "But, maybe. Camila is that good."

Bill stepped forward and reached out to shake Guillermo's hand. "I appreciate your hospitality, sir," Bill began. "I'm fortunate to be a guest in your home."

"Any friend of Marcheline's is a friend of mine," Guillermo replied. "No questions asked."

"Good," Bill said. He leaned forward so he could speak quietly, without the others overhearing. "I'm waiting on an important phone call tonight. Maybe two. Hopefully, the news I receive will help untangle Marcheline's... Situation. Do you mind if I step outside when my phone rings?"

"Not a problem," Guillermo confirmed, placing one hand on Bill's shoulder. "You do your thing. Do you really think you can help her?"

"I do. And I'm not going to give up easily. She's suffered for far too long."

Marcheline followed Camila into the kitchen, leaving the others space to talk about her further.

Sabine began. "Mr. Guillermo…"

"Just Guillermo. We're all friends here."

"Guillermo," she continued. "Mom told me what you were willing to do for us. I want to thank you. After today, I'm hopeful it won't be necessary. But I appreciate your kindness, anyway. You're a good man."

"Of course," Guillermo said emphatically. "Marcheline is a special friend of mine. I promised her many years ago now, when we were in college together, that if she ever needed me, I would step up. It didn't matter how many years had passed. My word is my bond."

Sabine leaned closer to Guillermo, and talked quietly, just like Bill had. "I've arranged a surprise for Mom tonight. Do you mind?"

"Not at all," Guillermo said. "Mi casa es tu casa… My home is your home."

Sabine thanked Guillermo again, then followed her mother and Camila into the kitchen, baby Amelie riding on her hip.

Ryan looked at Guillermo, and Guillermo laughed because Ryan clearly had something to say, too. Ryan leaned forward and talked quietly just like Bill and Sabine had. "Guillermo, sir…"

"Just Guillermo."

"Okay, Guillermo," Ryan continued. "I have something for Marcheline tonight."

"A surprise?" Guillermo said, getting a kick out of the various plans that were afoot.

"Well, yes," Ryan confirmed. "Do you mind?"

"Not in the slightest," Guillermo said. "Mi casa es tu casa… My home is your home. It should be an interesting night."

"I hope so," Ryan agreed. "It ought to be memorable."

Guillermo continued to smile as he opened the wine and poured glasses for everyone. He made a big deal of how good it tasted, complementing Marcheline on her company's products.

"I always knew you would go far, Marcheline Fay," Guillermo said as he pointed to his friend from across the room. "This girl is a go-getter, folks. She has been since a very long time ago. She's strong in a way that not many people are."

Camila nodded her partial understanding, then Guillermo translated for her in Spanish. Once she got the entire message, her face lit up, and she smiled as big as her husband. It seemed like Guillermo had told her about his friend Marcheline before.

"You're right about that," Bill said. "I've only known Marcheline for a day, and I can already tell she's exceptional. Like a diamond, formed under pressure and unpleasantness, but what an exceptional thing to behold. Marcheline is the picture of perseverance and determination. I'll bet she inspires everyone who knows her."

"She does," Sabine said proudly, sitting on a barstool

and bouncing Amelie on her knee. "She's amazing. I'm really proud that she's my mom."

Marcheline was tempted to brush off the praise as was her default response, but she didn't. For a change, she let herself take it in, feeling the love from her people. "You're very kind," she said. "The feeling is mutual. I have the best people."

"So, they all know now?" Guillermo asked.

"They do. They know even more than you," Marcheline said, then she filled her friend in on the missing pieces.

She told Guillermo about Huey and the abuse, and how she'd accused Chester as a way to set herself and Sabine free. It felt hard telling the story for a third time in one day, but every time she spoke it, and every time she spoke Huey's name, it got easier. Huey had less power over her the more she brought him out rather than keeping him hidden. She thought maybe it was true what people said about how monsters live in the dark. Once you shine a light on them, they aren't so scary anymore.

Guillermo walked over and wrapped his arm around Marcheline's shoulders. "I'm so sorry that happened to you," he said. Then he looked at his wife and spoke just one word that conveyed his message. "Violación."

Camila gasped, then walked over to Marcheline and embraced her from the other side. Marcheline wasn't used to people being so forward and generous, but in this setting, it felt good. It felt right.

"Thank you."

"You know, Marcheline," Guillermo continued. "You could have told me back then. I could have handled it."

"Guillermo, my darling, I don't know if *I* could have handled it. It was my issue. My hangup. You are a good friend to me. Don't you feel badly about it. You're one of the best friends I've ever had. Look at us now, all these years later and you were ready to get me a new identity, even if that meant getting me across the border to Mexico. If friends get any better than that, I don't know about it."

They all laughed.

"We were going to Mexico?" Bill asked, half joking and the other half serious.

"If necessary," Marcheline said. "But I don't think it will be necessary, thanks to you, Bill."

"Phew," Bill said, wiping his brow for dramatic effect. "I'm not sure how well I'd do in Mexico."

Camila looked at Guillermo for translation. "No habla español."

They laughed together again, Camila in on the joke this time.

The group continued to chat as Camila brought out finger foods and served them to her guests. They were decadent, the most delicious anyone present had tasted, by a long shot.

"Camila, my darling," Marcheline began. "You should open a restaurant. Your food is outstanding. Your restaurant would stay busy all the time."

Guillermo translated and Camila blushed when she understood. "Gracias," she said, several times.

The evening was going very well. Marcheline was more relaxed than she'd been in a long time as she continued to explain to Guillermo what she'd been doing over the past two days. He agreed it was strange to think she'd been at her office yesterday afternoon in Northern California, going about her business as if nothing was wrong.

Camila had just put on some mood music when the doorbell rang. It took a few rings before they heard it, but when they did, both Sabine and Ryan stood up and offered to go answer. Guillermo looked perplexed, but didn't mind allowing whatever was to unfold.

"Go ahead," he told them. "Let me know if you need anything."

Sabine handed Amelie to Marcheline and then followed behind her husband to the front door. Marcheline continued with her conversation and sips of wine, so didn't notice when it took the kids a while to return. When they did, they had someone special with them.

"Mom," Sabine said. "Someone is here to see you."

Marcheline turned, startled at first, until she saw her dear friend's smiling face. "Rande!" Marcheline yelled as she ran over to embrace him. "What in the world are you doing here?"

"I called him," Sabine said. "I thought you could use another friend today."

"And Ma'am, when Sabine told me what was going on," Rande added, "You had better believe I marched myself right onto a plane and got here as soon as I could."

"Oh, Rande," Marcheline said, in happy tears. "I wasn't sure I'd see you again. And here you are!"

"If you wanted to take a trip down here to damn near the Mexican border, all you had to do was ask," Rande said, laughing. "Charisse would have been happy enough to get rid of me for a few days."

Marcheline shook her head, laughing. She felt lighter and happier than she had in as long as she could remember. Before, there was happiness, but with sadness just underneath. Now, the sadness was starting to dissipate, like grains of sand being blown away or carried out by the tide. Whatever the mechanism, it was a wonderful feeling.

"Let me introduce you to everyone," Marcheline said, keeping one arm around Rande. "You know Sabine, Ryan, and Amelie, of course."

"Of course," Rande replied. "Hello, gang."

"And this is my dear friend, Guillermo Martinez, from college. He is my Plan A. I came here because he was going to help me change my identity. But I don't think I will do it, Rande. At least, it might not be necessary. I'm hopeful."

"Nice to meet you," Guillermo said as he shook Rande's hand. "This is my wife, Camila."

"Yes, the lovely Camila," Marcheline said. "She's a gracious host, a talented decorator, and an amazing cook. Wait until you try some of her food. It's delicious."

Guillermo translated for his wife, who blushed and smiled once she understood.

"Pleased to meet you," Rande said to Guillermo. "Anyone who takes care of our girl like you have is alright in my book."

"And this…" Marcheline began, gesturing towards Bill. "This is the man who called the office yesterday from Chicago."

"Yeah, isn't that the strangest thing?" Rande said. "Sabine told me the story."

"It is. What began as a frightening intrusion into my life has turned out to be one of the greatest gifts," Marcheline explained. "Bill has helped me so much already."

"And I'm working with a friend on the police force in Chicago to do plenty more," he said as he shook Rande's hand. "I'm expecting a call from him anytime now."

"Good man," Rande said.

"Mom," Sabine inserted. "You'll have to catch Rande up on Huey. I didn't tell him those details. I didn't feel like they were mine to tell."

"I appreciate that, Sabine," Marcheline said. "But you can tell Rande anything. Huey was too hard for me to talk about before, but now that it's out in the open, my friend Rande can know. Of course, he can know."

Sabine filled in the blanks, for which Marcheline was grateful. Even though it was getting easier, she was glad she didn't have to explain for a fourth time in one day.

"Ma'am," Rande said as he squeezed his friend tighter. "You know I'd do anything for you, right? And by the looks of it, you've got several other people who would say the same."

"I know, Rande. I do. I'm feeling that today more than ever. And I am incredibly grateful."

Guillermo smiled, pleased that his house could be the setting for this happy evening. He ushered everyone back towards the main living area, then poured Rande a glass of wine.

"House special?" Rande remarked, as proud of the

Maison du Vin wine as Marcheline. "So, now you know what fine wine this lady produces. The best in the wine country region, if I do say so myself. Hell, some of the best in the world."

They talked and laughed together, as Camila cooked the main dish in the oven. It was heavenly as the smell wafted throughout the home. Marcheline was enjoying herself in every moment, until suddenly, she noticed that Bill had disappeared.

Marcheline stood up straight, handing Amelie back to Sabine. She felt the familiar panicky feeling move across her body. Although this time, it was a little different. She trusted Bill. But she wasn't sure she had the fortitude to withstand the news he would receive from Chicago. If Huey was still a threat and had confirmed mob ties, all of her hopes for a normal life might be dashed. What if she had been right all along and the only way to keep her family safe was to run? She didn't want to run anymore. After the day she'd just had, she thought running away might just break her heart.

"Did his phone ring?" Marcheline asked.

30

"He must have stepped outside," Ryan said. "You stay here, Marcheline. I'll go check on him."

Guillermo looked curious. Having heard about the surprises Sabine and Ryan had planned and the calls that Bill expected to receive, he wondered what else the night would hold.

"Let him go," Guillermo said. "You stay here and relax, Marcheline. Ryan will let us know if there's anything notable."

Marcheline tried. She sat on Guillermo and Camila's sofa and did her best to remain there. What she really wanted to do was to jump up and run outside, then hang on Bill's every word. She wanted him to put Gary on speakerphone, so she could hear all the details. But she knew that she needed to act mature. Bill was helping her, after all. She knew he would tell her when he found out something useful.

But Marcheline didn't last long at all before she did jump up and run outside. She simply couldn't help it. "I'm sorry, Guillermo," she said. "I've got to know. I've been waiting a lifetime for this. I can't wait a minute more." She rushed out the front door and onto the wide, ample porch as the city lights twinkled in the distance. Bill was there, holding his new phone to his ear. Ryan was standing beside him.

"Okay, good deal," Bill said into the receiver. "Will do. Thanks, buddy." Then he hung up.

Marcheline rushed towards him, nearly knocking him down. She felt clumsy, like she had the day before when she had raced out of her office. "What did he say?" she asked, passion in every note of her voice.

Bill smiled from ear to ear. "Do you want me to tell you now, or inside with everybody else?"

"Wait," Ryan said. "I know Sabine will want to be here for this. Rande and Guillermo, too."

"Be here for what?" Sabine asked from over Marcheline's shoulder. Unable to wait any better than her mom, she had come outside. Amelie smiled cheerfully as she bobbed on Sabine's hip.

"What's that again?" Rande asked from behind Sabine. "You know I don't want to miss whatever's happening. I just flew all the way from California for this."

"And I don't want to miss it either!" Guillermo said, standing at the back of the group with Camila.

Marcheline looked at Bill. She knew she was about to receive news that would change her life. She was ready. "Tell me."

"Marcheline," Bill began as he put one hand on her shoulder. "I want you to know. I've been doing this for a long time. Not all stories have a happy ending…"

Marcheline was hanging on his every word. It was torture.

"But yours does."

The group erupted in cheers behind Marcheline, giving each other high fives and jumping up and down. It sounded more like a sports bar than the front porch of a Tucson home. The energy was contagious. Marcheline imagined herself as the girl about to be hoisted in the air at a concert and carried by the crowd.

"Tell me," she said again.

"That was Gary from Chicago. He looked into Huey Moreau, just like I asked him to."

Marcheline's heart seemed to stop dead in its tracks, then race, alternately. Her body felt all mixed up. It didn't know what to do any more than she did.

"Wow," Ryan said quietly, one arm around his wife. "Just wow."

"And?" Marcheline prompted.

"Are you ready for this?" Bill asked with a big smile.

"My God, Bill!" Marcheline exclaimed. "Yes. Get on with it."

"Huey Moreau of Evanston Illinois, owner of Moreau Jewelry, died fifteen years ago. He had a stroke and passed away in his sleep. He had no known ties to organized crime."

Marcheline fell to her knees with a gentle thud and put her head in her hands. Her whole body ached with relief. It was a good ache. A primal ache. It felt like she was an impala who had just escaped a brush with a tiger. She was *alive*. Her family and friends circled around her and squatted down beside. They put their arms on each other's shoulders, instinctively, and it felt to Marcheline like some kind of ancient ritual. It was a touching show of support.

When she gathered enough strength to speak again, Marcheline looked at Bill. "Thank you, from the bottom of my heart. This means everything to me. It's everything in my life. It's my... Freedom."

"That's not all," Bill said.

"There's more?" Sabine asked.

"Yes, young lady. And it concerns you."

Marcheline looked at Bill, her eyes pleading.

"It's okay Marcheline," he said to her. "I told you. Your story has a happy ending."

"Wait," Sabine said. "They didn't get the DNA test back already, did they? That would be super fast."

Bill removed his hands from the circle and clapped them in front of him. "They sure did! I told the concierge at the hotel to spare no expense in getting your sample there as soon as possible. They had it flown up this afternoon. When it arrived, Gary had the lab on standby for rush processing. They had pulled Chester's DNA, which was already in their system."

"I think I might faint," Sabine said. "I've been waiting for this for such a long time." She leaned on her husband and held her baby tightly as she looked at her mom.

"Are you ready?" Bill asked.

"Yes, yes, I really am," Sabine replied.

"And are you?" he asked Marcheline.

"Yes. Go ahead."

"Sabine Fay, results are conclusive with 99.9% accuracy. Chester Loor is your biological father. These results exclude Huey Moreau. That evil is gone from your lives forever. He can't hurt you anymore. And Chester is a good man. He's going to be thrilled to learn that he has a daughter."

"A daughter conceived out of love," Marcheline added, tears streaming out of her eyes. "Not abuse."

31

The celebration continued on Guillermo's porch. Marcheline couldn't put into words how wonderful she felt. A great burden had been lifted. It was a relief she thought would never come, so she didn't say anything, but let herself sit silently with her feelings. The others passed her from one person to the next, and held and rocked her like she was a baby. It was the most beautiful and touching thing Marcheline had ever witnessed, let alone been a part of. They stroked her hair, patted her back, and cradled her head as they leaned her on their shoulders. They attended to Sabine, too, patting and embracing her as she cried with the relief of finally knowing who her father was.

When they were all hugged and cried out, everyone made their way quietly inside, just in time for Camila's dinner to be served. She had made tacos, burritos, and enchiladas that were far better than any restaurant. The group continued to drink, and they shared happy stories and wishes for the future as they ate, handing baby Amelie between them.

As the conversation went on into the evening, Guillermo and Camila filled Marcheline in on everything they'd been doing. One of the highlights of the night for Marcheline was learning that Guillermo and his wife were in the process of adopting a baby. She'd always thought he would be a good dad, and she'd wondered why he didn't have kids already. Guillermo's courage to add a child to his life at their age was especially touching to Marcheline. It gave her hope for her own new beginnings. It made her feel like anything was possible.

Marcheline's head was still spinning, and she hadn't made plans for what she would do tomorrow, let alone for the rest of her life. But she noticed that Ryan kept looking at the clock on the wall. She thought maybe he was tired and wanted to get back to the hotel to get some more sleep. He had driven all night prior. Marcheline also noticed that Guillermo and Ryan kept making eye contact, as it Guillermo was in on whatever it was that Ryan was thinking about.

When the doorbell rang, they both shot up and out of their chairs.

"I'll get it!" Ryan said as he ran towards the front door.

"What is going on with him?" Marcheline asked. "Is he having something delivered? Because everybody's already here."

"It's a surprise!" Guillermo said as he followed closely behind.

"What?" Sabine asked, clueless as to what her husband was up to.

Rande leaned back in his chair and smiled. "This

should be good," he said. "Never a dull moment with you. Is there, Ma'am?"

"Apparently not," Marcheline replied. "Although, I don't know what to make of this. I don't know what's happening."

As the door opened and Ryan said hello, Marcheline heard a familiar, sweet voice. It sounded... Older than she remembered. But she'd recognize it anywhere. It was the voice that had sung her to sleep at night. The voice that had read her bedtime stories.

"Ryan?" the voice asked. Marcheline's heart nearly jumped out of her chest. "Thank you so much for your call."

"That's right," he replied. "I'm Ryan. I'm glad you made it. Come in."

Then a second familiar voice sounded. This one deeper and stronger, but just as loving.

"We're glad to be here."

Marcheline stood up, in a complete shock of the best kind, and waited for her eyes to see what her ears had heard. The others looked at her, confused, but they stood up with her as they awaited the guests slowly walking from the front door into the living room. Marcheline's people circled around her again, Rande taking one of her hands and Sabine the other, while Bill stood behind her and put a hand on her back, a symbolic gesture of his support.

And there, in front of Marcheline's eyes, were her beloved parents. Francine and Jean-Claude were alive, in the flesh, and standing in Guillermo's Tucson home, their faces beaming with love and pride.

ENJOY THIS BOOK?

A NOTE FROM AUTHOR KELLY UTT

Did you enjoy this book? You can make a big difference.

Reviews are the most powerful tools in my arsenal when it comes to getting attention for my books. As much as I'd like to, I don't have the financial muscle of a New York publisher. I can't take out full page ads in the newspaper or put posters on the subway.

(Not yet, anyway.)

But I do have something much more effective than that, and it's something that those publishers would kill to get their hands on.

A committed and loyal group of readers.

Honest reviews of my books help bring them to the attention of other readers.

If you've enjoyed this book, I would be very grateful if you could spend just five minutes leaving a review (it can be as short as you like) on the book's Amazon page and on Goodreads or BookBub.

Thank you very much.

ABOUT THE AUTHOR

Standards of Starlight Books
Kelly Utt

Kelly Utt writes emotional novels for readers who enjoy both suspense and sentimentality. She was born in Youngstown, Ohio in 1976.

Kelly grew up with a dad who would read a book on a weighty topic, ask her to read it, too, and then insist they discuss it together, igniting her passion for life's big questions. That passion is often reflected inKelly's novels, giving them a depth which leaves readers wanting more and thinking about her stories long after the last lines are read.

Kelly holds a Bachelor's degree in psychology from the

University of Tennessee, Knoxville and she studied graduate-level interactive media at Quinnipiac University.

She lives in the Nashville suburb of Franklin, Tennessee with her husband and sons.

www.kellyutt.com

desperate to keep her family together, Bea must identify and silence the person who stands in the way of her happiness.

Her Boldest Lie

Marcheline Fay claimed the father of her child wasn't in the picture. Now her daughter is all grown up and asking questions. When a decades-old letter gets mailed without Marcheline's permission, the lie she told might not be enough to keep them safe. Scrambling to find out who knows what and at risk of losing it all, Marcheline must reopen old wounds to make things right.

Her Darkest Hour

Her Buried Secret

Her Worst Mistake

———

In the George Hartmann Series

Psychological Thriller

The twisty George Hartmann Series chronicles the Hartmann and Davies families across time and space. This life-affirming story, anchored by the deep affection between George and Alessandra, reveals how the connections we share can ground us during even the most difficult times as we endeavor to learn what we're made of.

Join the family you'll feel like you already know as, together, they explore the meaning of life beyond what lies on the surface and fight to keep each other safe.

When George Met Ali

(Short Story Prequel)

George Hartmann is living like a typical twenty-something bachelor in the early aughts until one careless romp between the sheets lands him in a troublesome situation. In this prequel short story, you'll meet a young, twenty-something George Hartmann and you'll see how he nearly missed out on one of the very best things life had to offer.

Free to Download exclusively at Kelly's website

Ithaca's Soldier

When George Hartmann's past life as an Ancient Greek soldier catches up to his new life in Upstate New York, a violent break-in endangers his sons and brings the terrifying realization that centuries-old demons may be back to haunt. Will George be able to protect the ones he loves and find lasting peace?

Subject to Danger

A killer is on the loose. He murdered George Hartmann's boy when they lived a past life together in Ancient Greece, and he tried to do it again right here in the present. Will George put the pieces together in time, before ancient history repeats itself?

Places Blue

George Hartmann is at a breaking point. His three little boys have suffered one harrowing ordeal after another and now his wife's life hangs in the balance. The danger is real. There's little to go on besides a string of distant, pieced-together memories. And there's no place to hide.

Limits of Protection

There's an imminent threat to national security and George Hartmann is one of only a handful of patriots who can thwart it. The timing couldn't be worse. George is embroiled in a fight to keep his loved ones safe from ruthless villains who are determined to rehash a centuries-old vendetta. Will he find a way to navigate divided loyalties and save the day?

The Pieces

George Hartmann thought he'd seen rock bottom. It turns out he wasn't even close. Faced with impossible stakes on multiple fronts, he must pick up the pieces and forge a path forward.

Coming in 2020

————

Be the first to know when new books are released by signing up for Kelly's e-mail list at www.kellyutt.com.

The Rosemary Run Series is ongoing. Books can be read in any order.

The George Hartmann Series will continue with Book Five, *The Pieces*. Book are best read in order.

Kindle Unlimited Subscribers read for free.